"There's Something A[bout] [You That I] [Can't] Look Away, A[nd]..."

"You must have an iron will because you don't have any problems doing it."

He leaned forward, his arms resting on his knees and his face more sincere than Jessi had seen in a while. "That's because I'm not a sap. I know better than to let you think there is anything between us. You'd use it to get whatever you wanted."

She shrugged—it would be nice to believe she had that kind of power over him. "Good thing I stopped believing in fairy tales a long time ago."

"Sometimes I don't know whether to arm wrestle you or kiss you."

"Kiss me? That didn't really get us anywhere the last time," she said.

"I was hesitant because of business complications, but now there is nothing stopping me from taking what I want."

"Except me," she said softly.

She looked over at him to gauge his reaction and it was clear that he took it as a challenge.

* * *

Bound by a Child
is part of the Baby Business trilogy: One hostile takeover, two feuding families, three special babies

* * *

If you're on Twitter,
tell us what you think of Harlequin Desire!
#harlequindesire

Dear Reader,

Jessi and Allan! They are like oil and water: from the moment they met they just didn't like each other. Or at least that's what each wants the other to believe.

When I first realized what was going to have to happen to bring Jessi and Allan together I felt sad inside. And as I started writing Jessi and Allan's story, it became clear to me that the moment they learned that they'd be raising Hannah changed them both.

The fighting they'd always done began to seem superficial to each of them as the deaths of their best friends forced them to realize what was important in life. Jessi and Allan are still bantering back and forth and trying to figure out how to deal with a baby, but there is a new bond between them now.

I hope you enjoy *Bound by a Child*.

Happy reading!

Katherine

BOUND BY A CHILD

KATHERINE GARBERA

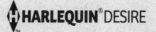

Recycling programs for this product may not exist in your area.

ISBN-13: 978-0-373-73299-9

BOUND BY A CHILD

Copyright © 2014 by Katherine Garbera

Printed in U.S.A.

Books by Katherine Garbera

Harlequin Desire

Silhouette Desire

Other titles by this author
available in ebook format.

KATHERINE GARBERA

is a *USA TODAY* bestselling author of more than forty books who has always believed in happy endings. She lives in England with her husband, children and their pampered pet, Godiva. Visit Katherine on the web at www.katherinegarbera.com, or catch up with her on Facebook and Twitter.

Huge thanks to all of the readers
who chat with me on my Facebook page,
especially Danny Bruggemann, Jean Gordon,
Barbara Padlo, Angie Floris Thompson and
Amelia Hernanadez, who suggested names
for the hurricane in this book. I ended up
choosing Pandora since it sort of fitted my story. :-)

Plus a shout-out to my U.K. writing buddies
Celia Anderson and Lucy Felthouse.
Thanks for talking books, hotties and UK phrases
with me. Writing is a hard, lonely job
and I have to thank my darling husband
and kiddos for their support. And as always
thanks to my editor, Charles, for his insight.

One

Allan McKinney might look like a Hollywood hottie with his lean, made-for-sin body, neatly styled dark brown hair and piercing silver eyes that could make a woman forget to think. But Jessi Chandler knew he was the devil in disguise.

He was the bad guy and always had been. More tempting than sin itself as he rode in at the last minute to ruin everything. Knowing him the way she did, she couldn't imagine he had come to her table in the corner of Little Bar here in the Wilshire/La Brea area of Los Angeles for any other reason than to crow about his latest victory.

It had been only three weeks since he and his vengeful cousins at Playtone Games had taken over her family's company, Infinity Games, bringing their longtime rivalry to a vicious climax.

She'd just come from a meeting at Playtone Games where she'd made a proposal to try to save her job. The most humiliating thing about this merger was having to grovel in front of Allan. She was a damned fine director of marketing, but instead of being able to continue in her role and just get on with the work that needed to be done, she had to trek into the city from Malibu once a week and prove to the Montrose cousins that she was earning her paycheck.

He slid into the booth across from her, his long legs brushing against hers. He acted as if he owned this place and the world. There was something about his arrogance that had always made her want to take him down a notch or two.

It was 5:00 p.m., and the bar was just beginning to get busy with the after-work crowd. She was anonymous here and could just let her guard down for a minute, but now that Allan was sitting across from her, messing with her mojo, that wasn't going to happen.

"Are you here to rub it in?" she asked at last. It fit with the man she believed him to be and with the little competition they'd had going since the moment they'd met. "Seems like a Montrose-McKinney thing to do."

Her father had been adamant about staying away from Thomas Montrose's grandsons due to the bad blood between their families. She got that, but even before the takeover, she'd had no choice but to deal with Allan when her best friend, Patti, had fallen in love with and married his best friend.

"Not quite. I'm here to make you an offer," he said, signaling the waitress and ordering a Glenlivet neat.

"Thanks, but I don't need your kind of help," she said. She'd probably find herself out of a job quicker with him on her side.

He ran his hand over the top of his short hair, narrowed his eyes and looked at her in a way that made her sit up straighter in her chair. "Do you get off on pushing me to the edge?"

"Sort of," she said. She did take a certain joy in sparring with him. And she kept score of who won and who lost.

"Why?" he asked, pulling out his iPhone and setting it on the table next to him. He glanced down at the screen and then brought his electric gaze back to her.

"Concentrating on your phone and not on the person you're with is one reason," she answered. It irked her when anyone did that, but bothered her even more when the person was Allan. "Besides, I like getting to see the chinks in your perfect facade when you can't hide the real Allan."

The waitress delivered his drink. He leaned forward on his elbows. The woman was thin and pretty and wore a pair of large black glasses that were clearly a personality statement and went well with her pixie haircut. Allan smiled at her, and the waitress blushed, which made Jessi roll her eyes.

"What did I do to make you so adversarial toward me?" he asked, turning back to her as the waitress left.

"Why do you care?"

"I'm tired of always arguing with you. In fact, that brings me back to my reason for tracking you down," he said.

"What reason?"

"I'd like to buy you out. Your shares in Infinity Games are now worth a lot of money, and we both know you don't want to work for my cousin Kell or me. I'll make you a fair offer."

She sat there in shock as his words sank in. Did he think her family heritage meant so little to her? When she thought of how her dad and grandfather had always been so busy at work that they'd never been around...

well, hell, no, she wasn't selling. Especially not to a Montrose heir. "Never. I'd give them away before I sold to you."

He shrugged. "I just thought I'd save all of us a lot of frustration. You don't seem to be really interested in working for the merged company."

"I'm not selling," she said one more time, just in case he had any illusion that she was going to walk away easily. "I'm planning to keep my job and make you and your cousins eat your words."

"What words?"

"That Emma and I are expendable. Don't deny that you believe it."

She and her older sister still had to prove themselves if they wanted to keep their jobs. Sure, they were shareholders, so they'd always have an ownership stake in the company, but their actual jobs were on the line. Their younger sister, Cari, had already jumped through hoops for the Montrose cousins and had ended up keeping her position and falling in love with one of them.

Declan Montrose was now engaged to her, though three months ago he'd arrived at Infinity Games to manage the merger of the two companies, which meant he was there to fire the Chandler sisters. But Cari had turned the tables on him, revealing that he was the father of her eighteen-month-old son as a result of a brief affair they'd had. This had been a big surprise to everyone on both sides of the merger. It had been an interesting time, to say the least, but in the end she and Dec had fallen in love and Cari had managed to save her job at the newly merged Playtone-Infinity Games.

"I wasn't going to deny it," Allan said. "The situation with both you and Emma is different than the one with

Cari. When she approached Dec and I with her ideas for saving the staff at Infinity Games she was happy to listen to our ideas, as well."

His words hurt; Jessi wasn't going to lie about that. But Cari was known for being the caring sister, and Jessi, well, she'd always been the rebel, the ballbuster. But that didn't mean she was emotionless. She wanted to see her family's legacy in video games continue; after all, Gregory Chandler had been a pioneer in the industry in the seventies and eighties. "I have a few ideas that I've been working on."

"Share them with me," Allan invited, glancing again at his phone.

"Why?" she asked.

"To see if you're sincere about wanting to keep your position. No more lame ideas like sending out Infinity-Playtone game characters to make appearances at malls. You're head of marketing and we expect more than that."

"It wasn't—" she said, but in her heart she knew it sort of was. She didn't want Playtone-Infinity to be successful so she'd...shot herself in the foot. "Okay, maybe it was a little lame."

"What else do you have in mind? You're too smart not to have something big," he said, staring at her with that intense gaze of his.

"Was that actually a compliment?"

"Don't act so surprised. You're very good at your job and we both know you know it. Talk to me, Jessi."

She hesitated. She *was* good, and she wasn't ever as tentative as she felt right now. It was just that she'd been beaten and felt like it today. "I don't... What can you do?"

"Decide if it's worth my time to help you," he said at last.

"Why?"

"Our best friends are married and we're their daughter's godparents. I can't just let Kell fire you without at least making some sort of effort to help," he said. "Patti and John would never forgive me."

"Then why offer to buy me out?"

"It would solve the problem and we'd both be able to walk away from this."

"It would," Jessi said. "But that's not happening."

She rubbed the back of her neck. She didn't like anything about this merger but she also didn't relish the idea of being fired. "I'm one person who wouldn't be swayed by your bank account."

He shrugged off her comment and for a moment looked pensive.

"It bothers you that I sent the jet to pick you and Patti up that first time we met, doesn't it?" he asked, leaning back and glancing at his iPhone, but quickly looking back at Jessi, which earned him a few more points toward being a good guy.

She took a swallow of her gin and tonic. "Yes. It felt like you were trying too hard. I mean, offering your private jet to fly us to Paris…that was showing off."

"Maybe I just wanted Patti to have a proposal she'd always remember. You and I both know that John doesn't earn what I earn. I was just helping my friend out."

"I know. It was romantic. I admit I didn't behave as well as I could have…. I guess I can be a bit of a brat."

"Well, you certainly were that weekend," he said,

leaning in so that she caught a whiff of his spicy aftershave.

She closed her eyes for a minute and acknowledged that if she didn't keep Allan in the adversary category, there was a part of her that would be attracted to him. He was the only person—man or woman—she'd ever met whom she could go head-to-head with and still talk to the next day. He understood that winning was important to her and didn't get mad when she won. He just got even, which, to be fair, appealed to her as much as it irritated her.

"But that's in the past. Let's work together. I think you and Emma probably have a lot to contribute to the newly merged company."

"Probably? Jeez, that sounds encouraging," she said, taking another sip of her drink.

"I'm trying here," he said.

"Well, I've got a few feelers out in the movie industry. There are three new action movies coming next summer that I think are good matches for the type of games that we develop, which might be enough lead time to get a really good game out." Given that the merged company was not only a prime video game developer for consoles like Xbox and PlayStation, but also had a thriving app business for smartphones and tablets, making games with movie tie-ins was a naturally good idea. Infinity Games had never pursued this line of business before, but since the takeover, Jessi and her sisters had been thinking outside the box.

"That's a great idea. I have some contacts in that area if you'd like me to use them," Allan offered.

"Really?"

"Yes," he said. "It's in my best interest to help you."

"Is it?"

"I'm the CFO, Jessi. Anything that affects the bottom line concerns me."

"Of course it does," she said.

She was torn. A part of her wanted to accept his help, but this was Allan McKinney, and she didn't trust him. It wasn't just that he'd thrown around his money as if the stuff grew on trees; it was also that she hadn't been able to find out much about him from her private investigator, whom she'd hired to check out John when Patti had first met him. What the detective had turned up about Allan...well, frankly, it had all seemed too good to be true.

No one had the kind of happy, pampered existence the P.I. had found when he dug into Allan's past. It was too clean, too...perfect. There was something he'd been hiding, but none of that had mattered at the time, since John McCoy was the main subject of the investigation and he'd turned out to be a good guy.

Maybe Jessi should ask Orly, her P.I., to start digging again. When it came to Allan, there had been too few leads and many closed doors the first time around. Given what had happened with Playtone and Infinity, and that she'd recently had Allan's cousin Dec investigated, too, maybe it was time to ask Orly to find out what more he could about Allan.

"Sure, I'd love your help," she said.

"You sound sarcastic," Allan commented, glancing down at his mobile phone yet again.

"It's the best I can do," she said.

"Excuse me for a moment. I keep getting a call from a number I don't know," he told her.

He picked up his phone and answered. After a moment, his brow furrowed, and he hunched back in his chair. "Oh, God, no," he muttered.

"What?" she asked. She grabbed her Kate Spade bag and started to slide off the bench, until Allan grabbed her hand.

She shook her head but waited as he listened, and then his face went ashen. He turned away from her.

"How?" he asked, his voice gruff.

She could only stare at him as he shook his head and rasped, "The baby?" After a pause he murmured, "Okay, I will be there on Friday." He disconnected the call and turned to her. "John and Patti are dead."

Jessi wanted to believe he was lying, but his face was pale and there was none of that arrogant charm she always associated with him. She pulled her phone out and saw that she, too, had received several calls from an unknown number.

"I can't believe it. Are you sure?"

He gave her a look that was so lost and wounded, she knew the truth.

"No," she said, wrapping her arm around her waist. *God, no.*

Allan was shaken to his core. He'd lost his parents at a rather young age, which was part of the reason he and John had bonded, but this was…wrong. It was just wrong that someone so young and with so much to live for had died.

Jessi's hands were shaking, and he glanced over at her, only to find everything he was feeling inside was there on her face. The woman who always looked so tough and in control was suddenly small and fragile.

He got up and moved around to her side, putting his

arm around her shoulder and drawing her into the curve of his body. She resisted for the merest of seconds before she turned her face into his chest, and he felt the humid warmth of her tears as they soaked into his shirt.

She was silent as she cried, which was nothing more than he'd expect from someone as in control as Jessi always was. By focusing on her pain and her tears he was able to bury his own feelings. A world without his best friend wasn't one he wanted to dwell on. John balanced him out. Reminded Allan of all the reasons why life was good. But now—

"How?" she asked, pushing back from him and grabbing a cocktail napkin to wipe her face and then blow her nose.

Her face was splotchy, red from the tears, and she took a shuddering breath as she tried to speak again. The tears were at odds with her rebel-without-a-care look. She wore her version of business attire, a short black skirt that ended at her thighs, a tight green jacket that had bright shiny zippers and a little shell camisole that revealed the upper curves of her breasts and her tattoo.

His chest was too tight for words. He didn't really know how to talk through the grief. But as he stared into those warm brown eyes of Jessi's—one of the very first things he'd noticed about her when they'd met—he realized that he could do this. He would pull himself together and do this for her.

"Car accident," he said.

"John is an excellent driver, as is Patti—oh, God, is Hannah okay?"

"Yes. She wasn't with them. Another driver hit them

head-on as they were coming home from a Chamber of Commerce meeting."

Allan was John's next-of-kin contact, which was why he'd gotten the call. "Let's get out of here."

She nodded. He could tell she was in no shape to drive, and steered her toward his Jaguar XF. She got into the passenger seat and then slumped forward, putting her hands over her face as her shoulders shook.

Never in his life had Allan felt this powerless, and he hated it. He stood outside the car and tipped his head back, staring up into the fading fall sunset. He felt tears burning in his own eyes and used his thumbs to press them back. He pushed hard on his eye sockets until he was able to staunch the flow, and then walked around the car and got inside.

Jessi sat there silently next to him, looking over at him with those wet, wounded eyes, and for the first time he saw the woman beneath the brashness. He saw someone who needed him.

"What is Hannah going to do? Patti's mom has Alzheimer's and there's no other close family."

"I don't know," he admitted. "John has some family but not really anyone close. Just a couple of cousins. We'll figure it out."

"Together," she said, meeting his gaze. "Oh, God. I can't believe I just said that."

"Me, either. But it only makes sense now."

"It does. Plus John and Patti would want us to do it together," Jessi said.

"Yes, they would," he said.

The little girl would never know her parents, but Allan decided he'd do everything in his power to ensure that she wouldn't grow up alone.

He took Jessi's hand in his. "Let's call their attorney back and find out the answers we both need."

She linked her fingers with his as he made the call and waited to be connected.

When he was put through, he said, "This is Allan McKinney again. You and I were just discussing John McCoy. Do you mind if I put you on speaker? I'm with Jessi Chandler. She is Hannah's other godparent."

"Not at all." Allan put the phone on speaker. "Go ahead."

"This is Reggie Blythe, Ms. Chandler. I'm the attorney for the McCoys."

"Hello, Mr. Blythe. What can you tell us?"

"Please call me Reggie. I don't have all the details as to what happened, but John and Patti were on their way back from a Chamber of Commerce dinner and were involved in a fatal accident. Miss Hannah was at home with a sitter—" they heard the rustling of papers "—Emily Duchamp. Emily has agreed to stay overnight with the baby. Hannah will be placed in a temporary foster situation in the morning."

Jessi's grip on Allan tightened. "Patti would hate that. Is there any way you can keep Hannah in her home?"

"Actually, as cogodparents, you have certain rights, but you will need to get here as soon as possible to avoid her being placed in the state's care."

State care. Allan knew that John never would have wanted Hannah to end up there. And there was no need for it. Didn't John have distant cousins and a great-aunt on his dad's side? "I believe John had a cousin who lives nearby."

"I don't think it's best to go into this over the phone. When can you both get to North Carolina?"

"As soon as humanly possible."

"Good," Reggie said. "I'll be in my office all day tomorrow. Please let me know when you two will get here."

"Oh, we're not together," Jessi said.

"Aren't you? You called me together, and given the terms of the will—never mind. We will sort it all out when you get to my office," Reggie said.

"Why did you think we were together?" Allan asked.

"John and Patti indicated in their will that they wanted guardianship to be given to the two of you."

"We figured as much," Jessi said. "We can come up with some sort of schedule."

"In the eyes of the courts," Reggie said, "the best arrangement is to provide a stable home for the child. But again, we can talk more about this when you get here."

When Allan disconnected the call, he dropped Jessi's hand, and she looked at him as if he'd grown two heads. "We fight all the time."

"We do," he said, before turning away and trying to think. It was almost too much to process.

His best friend was dead. Allan was a committed bachelor who had been named coguardian of a tiny baby with the one woman on the planet who aggravated him the most. He looked at her again. She seemed as upset by the tragedy as he was. But he knew they'd both do whatever they could to make the situation work. It didn't matter that they were enemies; from this moment forward they were bound together by baby Hannah.

"You and me…" she said.

"And baby makes three."

Two

Allan dropped Jessi off at her place in Echo Park. She looked small and lost and so unlike the indomitable woman he usually knew her to be that he didn't know how to handle her.

She didn't turn and wave as she entered her house, and he hadn't expected her to. He knew in time she'd get back to herself, but then he wondered if that were true. How could either of them ever be the same again?

Traffic was heavy, and it took him forty minutes to get to his home in Beverly Hills. He'd purchased the mansion after Playtone had made him a millionaire. John had actually helped him build the pergola and brick backyard eating area and barbecue. As he pulled into his circle drive, he was haunted by memories of his friend on his last visit to California.

Allan dropped his head forward on the steering wheel, but tears didn't come. Inside, he was cold and felt alone. And he realized that the last person he cared about was gone. He'd loved his parents, really loved them. They'd been a close family unit—just the three of them. Allan's grandfather had disowned his daughter when she'd refused to marry a wealthy heir he'd picked out for her, intending to funnel that money into his revenge against the Chandlers. It had only been after his grandfather's death when Kell had come to Allan and invited him to be a part of Playtone that he'd joined the company and put his penchant for managing money to good use.

She'd married instead for love, and they'd lived a quiet little life in the Temecula Valley—two hours away from Los Angeles, but really a world apart.

Allan heard a rap on the window of his Jaguar XF and looked up to see his butler, Michael Fawkes, standing there. The fifty-seven-year-old former middleweight boxer had been in his employ since he'd inked his first multimillion-dollar deal for Playtone. Fawkes was a great guy and looked a little bit like Mickey Rourke.

"Are you okay, sir?"

Allan took his keys from the ignition and climbed out of the car. "Yes, Fawkes, I am. But John McCoy was killed in a car accident. I'm leaving tomorrow to fly to the Outer Banks to help make funeral arrangements and see to his daughter."

"My condolences, sir. I liked Mr. McCoy," Fawkes said.

"Everyone liked him," Allan said.

"Shall I accompany you?" Fawkes asked.

"Yes. I need you to make sure we have accommodation in Hatteras. I think we should be able to stay at the B and B that John and Patti own…owned," he said, turning away from Fawkes. "Give me a minute."

Jessi would probably have a hard time booking a flight to North Carolina at this hour, and it wasn't a big town they were flying into. For a moment he rejected the idea of making an offer to let her fly with him. But then he knew he had to at least reach out to her. She was truly the only other person who felt the way he did right now.

As much as she irritated him, and though it irked him to admit it, he needed her. She made him feel as if he wasn't dealing with John's death alone.

"Please include Ms. Chandler in our arrangements," Allan said.

"Really?" Fawkes asked in a surprised tone of voice. Jessi did her best to rattle the butler whenever they came into contact.

"Yes. I was with her when she got the news. She's as affected by this as we both are."

Allan pulled his iPhone out of his pocket and texted her.

I'm taking the jet to North Carolina in the morning. Want a lift?

Jessi's response was immediate. Thanks. I'd appreciate that. Are you leaving tonight? I've made arrangements with the funeral home to talk about Patti's service in the morning. If we go tonight I can talk to them in person.

I had thought to leave tomorrow but given that we are going to lose three hours perhaps tonight is best.

I thought so.

Can you be packed and ready in two hours?

Of course. TTYL

"Very well, sir. I shall make all the arrangements," Fawkes said when he learned of the plan. "When are we leaving?"

"Two hours," Allan said.

He left his assistant and headed to his den, where he poured himself a stiff Scotch and then went over to his recliner to call his cousins. But there was a knock on the door before he could dial.

"Come in," he called.

Kell and Dec entered the room. They looked somber, and he realized that though John was his best friend, both his cousins had counted John as their friend, as well.

"We came as soon as we heard," Dec said. He stood in the doorway looking awkward.

"Thanks. I'm leaving tonight. I don't expect the trip to take more than a week. Jessi is coming with me, Kell. I think we might have to adjust some of her deadlines," Allan said. Even if she was his most irritating adversary, he had to help her out now. He'd seen her broken and he shared her pain.

"We can discuss business later. When will the funeral be?"

"I don't know. I have to talk to the funeral home once we get to North Carolina. John only had a few distant cousins. I won't know what kind of arrangements they might have already made until I'm on the ground there. I might end up in charge of the planning. And then there is Patti to consider. I know that Jessi is arranging her service."

"Just let us know and we'll fly out for it," Dec said. "Do you need anything?"

He shook his head. What could he say? For once he was at a loss for words. "I've got this," he finally said.

"Of course you do, but he was our friend, too," Dec said. Allan saw a quiet understanding in his cousin's eyes as he looked over at him.

Falling in love had changed the other man. He wasn't as distant as he'd always been.

"I don't know how else to handle this except to plan and take control," Allan admitted.

"That's the only way," Kell said. "We'll leave you to it."

Dec glanced quickly at him again as he followed Kell out. When his cousins were gone, Allan fell back on the large, battered brown sofa that didn't quite fit with the decor in the elegant and luxuriously appointed room. The couch had major sentimental value—John and Allan had purchased this piece at a garage sale for their first college apartment.

He put the heels of his hands over his eyes, pushing as hard as he could until he saw stars and there were no more tears.

"Another Scotch, sir?"

Allan dropped his hands and glanced up at his butler. Fawkes was standing there with a glass in one hand. "No. I'm going to pack and then get ready to head to the airport."

"Yes, sir," Fawkes said. "I have already arranged the accommodations. I've been tracking the weather, as well…. There might be a situation."

"What kind of situation?"

"Tropical storm in the Atlantic, but it's not predicted to head toward North Carolina. Just keeping my eye on it."

"Thanks, Fawkes."

Allan walked away and forced his mind to the task at hand. There was no reason why he couldn't get through his best friend's death the way he handled everything else. He'd manage and take control of the situation.

For once, Jessi's sharp tongue was dulled by Allan's generous offer to let her ride on his jet to the Outer Banks with him. Or maybe it was all the talk of funerals making her numb. As soon as she finished texting, she turned to put her phone on the hall table and found herself staring at a photo of Patti on the wall.

Jessi's heart hurt and she started to cry. She missed Patti. She missed the talks they wouldn't have. She longed to be able to pick up the phone and call her again. But that couldn't happen.

She sank to the floor, wrapped her arms around her waist and just sat there, trying to pretend that the news wasn't true. She didn't want to imagine her world without Patti. Granted, she had her sisters, but Patti was the person who knew her best. They'd gotten into trouble together since the second grade. What was she going to do now?

There was a knock on the door and she stared at it before forcing herself to her feet and wiping her face on her sleeve. Then she took a quick look at herself in the mirror.

Pitiful. Suck it, up, Jess. No one likes a crybaby.

"Coming," she called, but took a moment to wipe off the smudges that the combination of her tears and her heavy eyeliner had made on her face.

"We came as soon as we heard," Emma said when Jessi answered the ringing doorbell. Their youngest sister was there, too. Both women had their children with them. Emma's three-year-old Sam was holding his mother's hand, and twenty-one-month-old D.J. was sleeping quietly in Cari's arms.

"I didn't think you guys would get here so fast," Jessi said.

"Dec heard about it from Allan," Cari said, crossing the threshold and giving Jessi a one-armed hug. Jessi wrapped her own arms around her sister and nephew and held them close. Emma shut the door and joined the group hug.

Jessi felt the sting of tears once more, but choked them back. Though it was okay to let loose with her sisters, she didn't want to start crying again. Tears weren't going to bring Patti and John back. Tears weren't going to do anything helpful.

"What can we do?" Emma asked.

"I'm not sure. The funeral will have to be arranged, and then there is Hannah...."

"What about her?"

"Allan and I are her godparents. I agreed to it because Patti asked. But I'm not good with babies. You both know this. I'm just—" Jessi abruptly stopped talking. She wasn't going to admit to her sisters that she had no idea what to do next. For only the second time in her life she was lost. Lost. It was a place she'd vowed to never let herself be again.

Emma wrapped her arms around her again and for a minute Jessi was seven and her big sister's hug could fix all her problems. She hugged her sister back and took comfort from her before gathering herself and stepping away.

"I'm okay."

Cari looked skeptical, but was too nice to say any-thing. Emma just watched her, and finally Jessi turned on her heel and walked toward her bedroom. She could tell one of her sisters was following her, but didn't turn around to see who. If it was Cari, that would be fine. Cari would just accept whatever Jessi said and leave it be. But Em. Em had seen her share of heartbreak and had dealt with grief when she'd lost her young husband. Emma would be harder to keep her true feelings from.

"What bag are you taking?" Cari asked as she en-tered the bedroom without D.J.

Jessi breathed a sigh of relief and pretended it wasn't tinged with disappointment. She could have used a lit-tle of Emma's meddling right now. Something to rebel against instead of Cari's kindness.

"I don't know how long we'll be gone," Jessi said. "I need to leave some notes for my assistant, Marcel. My job is still on the line."

"Even Kell can't be that heartless. He'll give you some more time," Cari said. "I'll talk to him about it."

She nodded at her sister, but at this moment was too numb to get worked up about it. Patti was dead. That dominated every thought Jessi had.

"How about if I pack for you," Cari said. "You go talk to Marcel. Get everything sorted out before you leave."

"Thanks, Cari."

Her pretty blonde sister looked as if she was going to cry. For a minute, as Jessi gazed at her, with her neat preppy skirt, her tucked-in blouse and her hair in that high ponytail, she envied her. Cari had seen some rough times—giving birth to her son on her own after the father had abandoned her—but she'd found her own strength. That was what Jessi needed right now.

Work wasn't a solace for her the way that it had been for Emma when her husband died. And Jessi's personal life... Well, without Patti she didn't know what she was going to do.

She left her bedroom without another word, avoiding the living room, where she heard Emma talking to Sam and D.J. After listening a moment, Jessi made her way to her home office.

It was decorated with sleek modern furniture in bright primary colors. She sat down on her desk chair and opened her laptop to start sending emails.

As her system loaded messages and sorted them into different folders, she noticed the file labeled Patti had a new message. For some reason it hadn't downloaded to her phone, maybe because she'd turned off email during her meeting at the Playtone offices earlier in the day. As she reached for her phone and adjusted the settings, she started to cry. This would be the last message from Patti.

Jessi looked back at her laptop screen and hovered the cursor over the folder, afraid to open it. But after taking a deep breath, she clicked her mouse and read the email.

Can't wait to see you in two weeks. Here's a quick picture of Hannah. She's teething and that means her first tooth! And you, dear godmother, have to buy her a pair of shoes—according to my great-aunt Berthe. Hope everything is ok at work. I just know that you will figure it all out. Call me later.
Take care,
Patti

A photo of Hannah's little face filled the bottom of the screen. She had her fist in her mouth, there was a drool on her lips and she looked out from the picture with Patti's eyes. Jessi's heart clenched and her stomach roiled as she realized that her dear friend wasn't going to see that first tooth come in.

Since her door was closed and no one could witness it, she leaned her head on the desk and let herself cry.

As the plane lifted off, Allan watched Jessi put her earbuds in and turn away from him toward the window. To say that she wasn't herself was an absolute understatement. The woman who'd always irritated him was positively subdued. A shadow of her normal self. He saw her wipe away a tear in the reflection from the glass.

He knew it was none of his business. He owed Jessi next to nothing, and she was entitled to her grief. In fact, he understood completely how she felt, but a part of him wanted to needle her. Wanted to jar her and force her out of her funk so she could irritate him and he'd be able to forget. The last thing he wanted to do was spend a cross-country flight with his own thoughts.

Not right now when he was wondering why a confirmed bachelor was still alive and a family man with everything to live for was dead. God knew that Allan wasn't religious, and something like this just reinforced his belief that there definitely wasn't a higher force in the world. There was no fairness to John dying when he had so much to live for.

Allan looked around the cabin. He'd bought the G6 jet when Playtone had signed their first multibillion-dollar contract, and he didn't regret it. If there was one thing he prized in this life it was his own comfort. The cream-colored leather chairs had more than enough room for him to stretch out his six-foot, five-inch frame. He did so now, deliberately knocking over Jessi's expensive-looking leather bag in the process.

She glanced at him with one eyebrow arched and picked up the bag without removing her earbuds. She leaned her head back against the seat and a lock of her short ebony hair slid down over her eye. He had touched her hair once. It was cool and soft. He'd tangled his hand in it as he'd kissed her at John and Patti's wedding, behind the balustrade, out of the way of prying eyes.

Like everything between the two of them, he'd meant the kiss to be a game of one-upmanship, to shock her, but it hadn't worked. It had rocked *him* to his foundations, because there'd been a spark of something more in that one kiss. How was it that his archnemesis could turn him on like no other woman could?

He nudged her bag and she took her earbuds off as she turned to him and stared. Her gaze was glacial, as if he wasn't worth her attention.

"What's your problem?" she asked.

"Can't get comfortable," he said.

She glanced around at the six other empty seats before turning her chocolate-brown eyes back at him. "Really? Looks like you could stretch out and not bother me if you wanted to. So I ask again, what's your problem?"

"Maybe I want to bother you."

"Of course you do. What's the matter, Allan, finally found the one thing your money can't buy?" she asked.

"And what would that be?" he retorted. In his experience there wasn't much money couldn't afford him. Granted, it wasn't going to bring John back, but there was nothing that could stop death. And hadn't he learned that at an early age, anyway, when his mother had been the victim of a botched surgery?

"Peace of mind," Jessi said, swiveling her chair to face him and leaning forward so that the material of her blouse gaped and afforded him a glimpse of her cleavage.

She said something else, but all he could concentrate on was her body. Though she dressed in that funky style of hers she always looked well put together and feminine. And he couldn't help but recall the way she'd felt in his arms at John and Patti's wedding.

Dammit, man, enough. She's the enemy and it's just grief making her seem irresistible.

"I'll grant you that. Though I do find that my peace of mind is enhanced by the things I buy," he said.

"Me, too," she admitted.

"What do you want to buy right now?" he asked. He had already decided to order himself a Harley-Davidson, which he and John had been talking about buying when they turned thirty-five. Now that John was gone, Allan wasn't going to wait any longer. Life was too short.

"Nothing," she said. "I usually splurge on travel, and Patti was my…" She turned her chair to face forward.

"Not talking about her isn't going to make your grief any easier," he said softly.

She shrugged. "You're right. Maybe tomorrow I'll be able to think about this rationally, but tonight…I can't."

"Why?"

She turned to give him one of her you're-an-idiot-glares. "Seriously?"

"I don't want to sit in silence for the next few hours.

I keep thinking about John and Patti and how the last time I saw them both…"

"Me, too," Jessi said. "I can't stop. I remember how you and I were fighting, and Patti asked me to try to get along."

She stopped talking and turned away again to wipe a tear from her eye.

"John said the same thing to me. He even went so far as to mention that you weren't too bad," Allan said.

She shook her head. "I liked him. He was good for Patti and he loved her, you know?"

"He certainly seemed to." John had spent a lot of time talking about Patti, and Allan believed his friend loved her. But Allan had never experienced any emotions like that so it was a little hard to believe love existed.

"Seemed to? Don't you believe he loved her?" Jessi asked.

"I think he thought he did. But I'm not sure that love is real. I think it's something we all come up with to assure ourselves we're not alone."

She turned in her seat and arched both eyebrows as she leaned forward. "Even you can't be that cynical."

He shrugged. He didn't get the love thing between a man and a woman. He'd seen people do a lot of things out of "love" and not one of them had been altruistic or all that great. And his own experiences with the emotion had been haphazard at best.

Especially since he'd become a very wealthy man. Women seemed to fall for him instantly, and as Jessi would be the first to point out, he wasn't that charming. It made it very hard for him to trust them. But to be honest he'd always had trust issues. How could you believe in love when so many people did things for love that weren't all that nice?

"But you're always dating," she said. "Why do that if you don't believe in love and finding the one to spend the rest of your life with?"

"Sex," he said bluntly.

"How clichéd," she replied. "And typically male."

"Like your attitude isn't typically female? It's true I like women for sex. And companionship. I enjoy having them around, but love? That's never entered into the picture," he said.

"Maybe because you'd have to put someone else first," she suggested.

"I'm capable of doing that," he said, thinking of his friendship with John, but also his relationship with his cousins. He would go to them in the middle of the night if they called. Hence this cross-country red-eye to settle John's affairs. "What about you? You don't really strike me as a romantic."

"I'm not," she said. "But I do believe in love. I've got the heartbreak to prove that falling in love is real."

"Who broke your heart?" he asked. It was the first time in the five years he'd known her that she'd admitted to anything this personal. And he found himself unable to look away. Unable to stop the tide of emotions running through him as he stared at her. Who had hurt her and why did it suddenly matter to him?

"Some dick," she said.

He almost smiled because she sounded more angry than brokenhearted. "Tell me more."

"That's none of your business, Allan. Just trust me. If you ever let yourself be real instead of throwing around money and buying yourself trophy girlfriends, you'd find love."

He doubted it. "You think so? Is that how it happened for you?"

"Nah, I was too young and thought lust was love," she said. "Happy?"

"Not really," he said. "If you haven't experienced real love why are you so convinced it exists?"

"John and Patti. I've never met two people more in love. And as much as it pains me to admit it, your cousin Dec seems to be in love with my sister."

"They are borderline cutesy with all that hand-holding and kissing."

And just like that, she'd turned the tables and made him realize the truth of what she was saying. John was one of the few people he'd genuinely cared for, but they'd been friends for a long time, way before Allan had made his fortune and started running with the mon-eyed crowd. He didn't want to admit that maybe Jessi was right, but a part of him knew she was.

Three

She'd turned away after that conversation and he'd let her. Really talking about love with Allan wasn't something Jessi was truly interested in. The music on her iPod wasn't loud or angry—in fact, she was listening to the boy band 'N Sync. She and Patti had listened to their music endlessly when they were teens, and now the songs brought her some comfort. However, when "Bye Bye Bye" almost made her cry, she pulled her earbuds out of her ears and turned her attention to Allan.

He was restlessly pacing the length of the cabin and talking on the phone. She thought she heard him saying something about Jack White. She currently had a lead on the famous Hollywood director-producer and was trying to book a meeting with him later this month to discuss developing some of his summer blockbusters into games. It would be a coup if she could do a deal with Jack, and it would guarantee her job at Playtone-Infinity.

Allan glanced over and caught her staring.

"I'll have to call you back when we land."

He disconnected the call and pocketed his iPhone.

"We're playing for the same team now," she said. "You don't have to hide your business."

"You're on probation," he reminded her. "I'm not sure you'll make it past the ninety days."

"Really? I'm pretty sure I will. Have you ever known me to fail?"

He turned the leather chair in front of her to face her, and fell down into it. "Not without a hell of a fight."

She smiled. It almost felt like old times. They were finally finding their way back to their normal bickering, but she had the feeling they were both playing a role. Hell, she was. She was trying to be "normal" when everything inside of her was chaos.

"True dat."

"With all that's going on, we haven't had a chance to talk about my offer to buy you out," he reminded her. "I'm still willing to do that."

"I thought we'd already taken care of that. My answer remains no. I'm sorry if I've given you the impression that I'm someone who walks away from a difficult situation."

"Okay, okay. So what are you going to do to convince the Playtone board of directors to keep you on?"

Aside from doing a deal with Jack White, which was a long shot, she had no idea. Her plans for her future at the merged company were vague. It wasn't like her to be so wishy-washy, but she was tired of the entire family feud thing and was beginning to wonder if she even liked video games. She'd never admit that particular fact to a living soul. There were parts of the company that she loved, but right now she couldn't name them. There had been so much contention lately with the Montrose heirs that she hadn't been able to enjoy going to work.

"I am working on a push for Cari's holiday game. It will launch in two weeks' time and my team is working to make sure it's a hit."

Her sister and the development team had come up with an idea for a game app for the holidays that enabled players to decorate houses and Christmas trees, and then post screen shots to the online game center to try to get the most votes for their decor. The leaderboard was updated every day. The project had used existing assets at the company, so had a really low cost, and Emma believed it was that kind of out-of-the-box thinking that had saved Cari's job. It wasn't that there weren't other holiday apps; it was more the fact that Infinity Games had never done one before and that practically every component of the game was pure profit.

"That's good, but it won't be enough to save your job," he said.

She wished there was something easy or magical she could do to get herself out of this situation. But it was hard enough to be in this position, let alone having to come up with something so revolutionary it would impress the board at Playtone. It was going to take a lot to do that. Kell, Dec and Allan hated her grandfather and Infinity Games for what they'd done to old Thomas Montrose, and they wanted her to fail.

She held back a sigh—she'd never let Allan see that kind of weakness from her. "I'm not about to let you win. I don't care if I have to work 24/7 when we get back from taking care of this business on the East Coast. That's what I'll do."

He gave her that cocky half grin of his. "I expected a fight. Glad to hear you will be delivering one."

"Really?"

"Yes," he said. "I like our skirmishes."

"Is that all our encounters are to you?" she asked, thinking of that one kiss they'd shared. There was something weird about kissing your enemy and finding some attraction there.

"Are you asking about the night of Patti and John's wedding?"

"Yes. Seemed like we weren't at war that night."

"Well, we were, but we got distracted," he said.

"Until someone prettier came along," she said, remembering watching another bridesmaid, Camille Bolls, walk out of Allan's hotel room the morning after.

He shook his head. "There is no one who can compare to you."

"Ah, I've looked in the mirror. I'm not a classic beauty," Jessi admitted. And clearly not his type. It didn't bother her. Really, it didn't. She had chosen her look a long time ago and had done it deliberately. Most people saw her modern punk exterior and decided she was hard as nails. Exactly what she'd intended when she'd had her nose pierced and a small tattoo done on her collarbone near the hollow of her throat. It was discreet and could be covered with the collar of most blouses.

"No, but there is still…something about you that makes it hard to look away," he said.

"You must have an iron will because you don't have any problems doing it," she said.

He leaned forward, his arms resting on his knees and his expression more sincere than she'd seen in a while. "That's because I'm not a sap. I know better than to let you think there is anything between us. You'd use it, and me, to get whatever you wanted."

She shrugged. It would be nice to believe she had that kind of power over him. "Good thing I stopped believing in fairy tales a long time ago."

"Sometimes I don't know whether to arm wrestle you or kiss you."

"Kiss me? That didn't really get us anywhere the last time," she said.

"I was hesitant because of business complications, but now Playtone has the upper hand with Infinity and there is nothing stopping me from taking what I want."

"Except me," she said softly.

She looked over at him to gauge his reaction, and it was clear that he took it as a challenge. Suddenly, she was able to let herself forget about everything else that had happened today. Forget about the mess that her life was at this moment and remember that Allan McKinney was the one man who'd always been a worthy opponent.

"Except you," he said, "But I have a feeling you want to know if that one kiss was a fluke, as well."

"I have a feeling you're nothing but ego," she countered, refusing to let him see that she was intrigued. She'd never admit it out loud, but she'd had more than one hot fantasy about him.

She didn't really want to do this now, didn't want to have some kind of intense physical attraction to Allan McKinney. But there was no denying that she'd thought about that embrace more times than she'd wanted to over the past year and a half. She'd thought about *him* more than she'd wanted to. And those thoughts hadn't always involved fantasies of seeing him roasted over a pit.

She had to admit that in her musings he was usually shirtless, and most times they were both overheated. But that was her secret desire, and no way was she letting anything like that out in the open.

She looked so determined and at the same time so adorable.… What was wrong with him? Had he really become so bored with life that the only time he felt truly engaged was when he was going toe-to-toe with this woman? He could deny it all he wanted, but he knew the truth. There was something about Jessi that turned him on.

They were alone in the jet and would be for the entirety of the flight. Fawkes rode up front in the cockpit and functioned as copilot.

Allan had thought of Jessi as steel-hearted before today. She'd always seemed sort of a ballbuster until he'd seen the cracks and chinks in her tough-girl facade. Even when she'd hired that P.I. to investigate John before he'd married Patti, Allan hadn't realized that she'd done it because of her deep emotional attachments, not just to be a bitch. Because she cared about her friend… maybe even loved her. He'd never suspected that the woman who needled him the way she did could be as soft as he was beginning to suspect she was.

"I think I might be able to persuade you to come around to my way of thinking about sex instead of love," he said. He needed to change the dynamic between them. Get them back to the familiar footing they'd always been on.

"That's putting a lot of pressure on your charm and sex appeal," she said with a wry grin.

"Trying to take potshots at my ego?" He put his hand over his heart. "Hoping to see if you can deflate me?"

"Sort of. Is it working?"

"Nah, I still know I'm all that and a bag of dough-nuts," he said.

She laughed, but it sounded a little forced to him, and he realized she was on edge, too. Maybe because she'd felt something for him that one night, or maybe it still had to do with John's and Patti's deaths. Allan had no idea, and if he were honest, he didn't care at this moment. Thinking about Jessi, sparring with her, kept him from remembering his best friend was dead.

"You're some piece of work," she said. "Let's see what you're bringing to the game, big boy. How are you going to tempt me?"

"I thought I'd make it into a challenge," he said.

"What kind?"

She seemed intrigued, and he had to wonder if maybe she needed a distraction, the way he did. They'd always made bets over outrageous things and always honored them. In fact, if she weren't so…well, if she weren't *Jessi,* he'd actually like her. But she was Jessi. A Chandler. A prickly, ornery woman with as much cuddliness as a porcupine.

"One you won't want to lose," he said.

"I'm listening."

"I'm betting that you're attracted to me and that you can't control yourself better than I can when we put each other to the test," he said. It was a calculated risk. A chance to prove to himself that his iron willpower over his body and his sexual prowess were still intact. Because there was something very different about Jessi, something that he didn't entirely know how to deal with.

"I know I can," she said. "So what's in it for me?"

He thought about it for a few long minutes, shifting back in the chair. Just thinking of kissing her made him stir, so he stretched his long legs out in front of him to relieve the pressure on his groin.

"If you win I'll help you keep your job at the newly merged Playtone-Infinity Games," he said.

A light went out of her eyes and he saw her nibble on her lower lip. He didn't know what he'd said to cause that reaction, and made a mental note to pursue the question at another time.

"And if you win?" she asked.

"You let me buy you out," he said. "You walk away from gaming a wealthy woman."

"If you agree to help me, can you guarantee that I won't be axed?" she asked. "Because I don't think Kell is going to be that impressed with you saying that you lost a kissing contest with me and that's why you have to keep me on."

"Oh, Jess, I'm not going to lose," Allan said. "But if I do, I will help you by making my network of contacts available to you. I have a feeling that with those connections you'd be unstoppable."

"Why not just do that anyway?" she asked.

"We're enemies, remember? From the first moment we met you knew I was a Montrose cousin and I knew you were a Chandler sister."

"True. The family feud will always be there, won't it? Even though Cari and Dec have a son and are planning to get married…there's still bad blood between our families in your eyes."

"It's hard to just dismiss it," he said. "So do we have a deal?"

She crossed her arms under her breasts while she leaned back in her chair, then crossed her slim legs. She wore boots that would look ridiculous on anyone else, combat boots with a thick, three-inch heel that gave her added height. Tight-fitting leather pants and a loose, sheer black blouse completed the outfit. But it wasn't inappropriate, given that it was Jessi. He could tell by her all-black outfit that she was mourning.

"All I have to do to win is make sure you are more affected by one kiss than I am?" she asked.

"That's it. Keep in mind in certain circles I'm known as—"

"The man with a big mouth and bigger ego?" she taunted.

"You're going down, Chandler," he said.

"Only if I agree to your deal. And given how hard you're pushing for me to accept it, I'd say I'm destined to win."

"There was something destined to happen," he said, leaning forward in his chair and putting his hands on the armrests on either side of her. "Stop baiting me and make your choice."

"Am I baiting you?" she asked, shifting closer to him and tilting her head to one side as she stared at his mouth.

"You know you are," he said, trying to ignore the tingling of his lips. He was in control here.

"Well, then I guess I'm going to have to accept your wager. Prepare to lose, McKinney," she said.

Jessi came over to him and straddled his lap. Slowly, she eased forward and brought her mouth down on his. Her only thought was to do this and win, and then she'd focus on keeping her job. But the moment her mouth met his something changed.

It had been easy to tell herself that her memory of

what had happened between them at the wedding wasn't accurate, or that everything had been due to the champagne she'd drunk that night. But now, in the cold reality at thirty-five thousand feet in the air, there was no denying that the attraction she felt for him was real.

His mouth was firm against hers and his lips were soft. He was letting her be the aggressor, and she took full advantage of that, running her tongue over the seam where his lips met. He tasted minty and fresh, and she pulled back, but felt his hand on her head, keeping her in place.

His tongue traced her lips, as well, and she wondered if he'd like the flavor of her strawberry lip gloss or if it would be too sweet for him. But he didn't say anything, only kept coming back to taste more of it and of her.

She opened her mouth and felt the brush of his tongue over hers. She wanted to moan, but kept that sound locked away. She struggled to remember she was competing here. And suddenly it seemed stupid to her that the first man she'd kissed in a long time— and wanted to keep on kissing—was playing a game with her.

She closed her eyes and let herself experience the embrace of a man who made her want to forget she was a Chandler, and just enjoy being a woman.

His mouth was warm, and he tasted good. So good she never wanted the kiss to end. She shifted to get closer to him, but he kept the distance between them and she realized she was in danger of losing this bet. She hadn't anticipated having to fight her own urges while she kissed him.

She tried to think of Allan, tried to stem the need welling up inside her to feel his solid chest pressed against hers. Tried to forget that she'd seen him shirt-less enough times to know that he had solid pecs and a well-developed six-pack. Tried to forget that the man was seriously ripped.

She was losing it and losing the challenge. But then she felt the barest movement of his fingers against her neck. The tracing of a pattern that sent shivers down her spine and electric tingles through her entire body. *Dammit,* she thought, as every nerve ending started to pulse in time with her heartbeat.

She reached for his head. Tunneled her fingers through his thick hair and pulled him closer. She thrust her tongue deep into his mouth and forced him to take her. Reminded him that she was in control of this desire and this embrace.

But then he answered back and she was once again adrift. Forced to forget about wagers and feuds and every single thing except the way his mouth felt against hers and the way he made her wish this kiss would never end.

She rubbed her thumb against the base of his neck in a small circle and felt his heartbeat quicken. She took her time spreading her fingers out and enjoying the feel of his scalp under her hand, until she shifted forward and forced his head to the side, where she could take more control of their embrace.

But it was no longer about power or winning. Now she was kissing him because the taste of him was addictive. She'd never forget this one moment for years to come; she knew it with bone-deep certainty. The way he felt with just her hands in his hair and her lips on his. The way his tongue felt deep in her mouth as the smell of his aftershave surrounded her.

The dreams and desires she'd forced aside for too long came rushing up to her and she saw a chance to have everything she'd ever wanted. A man who could make her feel real desire and an out to walk away from the gaming world once and for all. All she'd have to do was give up everything she'd made herself into as an adult.

She'd have to lose to Allan. She'd have to show him that she could be vulnerable, and she'd have to admit it all out loud.

She sucked his lower lip into her mouth and bit down, and then rubbed her tongue over it to soothe it. She didn't think she could do that. But when she felt his hands tightening in her hair for a moment and a low groan issued from the back of his throat, she realized she might not have to.

He pulled his mouth from hers. She opened her eyes to look up into his intense gaze, and shook from what she saw there. He might want to pretend that she was nothing more than an old enemy to him, but the truth was there in those dilated pupils and in the flush across his cheekbones.

She almost cursed out loud as she realized there was no winner in this. No outcome that could be decided other than the truth. She was attracted to him. And though she'd hoped that maybe kissing him would distract her from the lonely feeling in her soul, it hadn't worked. In fact, she really wanted to just curl up next to him and forget about challenges and the world outside, and take some comfort in his arms.

If he hadn't made this a contest and if she'd been a different sort of woman—the kind who was okay being emotional and needy—then she'd be able to just rest her head on his shoulder and admit that she hadn't ever felt this scared and alone before.

"So…" he said. "That was more than I expected."

"Me, too," she admitted. "I guess we underestimated how much we'd enjoy each other."

"I sure did. Tonight especially, I…I enjoyed kissing you, Jessi."

"Me, too, Allan. I don't think you're my archnemesis anymore."

"That's good. So what are we going to do about this? Is it just grief? Did we turn to each other because our friends are gone?"

She shrugged. A part of her wanted to say yes and make this about the tragedy that had brought them both together. But she knew that would be a lie. And lying even to herself was something she didn't like to do.

"I really don't know," she admitted.

"Me, either. I have always been able to… Never mind. The real question is what are we going to do about it?"

She didn't have an answer. There wasn't a clear solution. He had surprised her and made her realize that there was more to this man than she'd previously thought. Because if he'd been all ego, then he would have swaggered away from her. But he was sitting across from her, looking just as perplexed as she was.

Four

It was humid and breezy as they stepped off the plane at the Dare County Airport in Manteo, North Carolina. Unlike the Los Angeles area, where everything was either developed or part of the desert, North Carolina—and especially the Outer Banks—was made up of small villages surrounded by state-owned land that had been preserved to keep this part of the world wild.

As the breeze flattened her shirt to her breasts, Allan was transfixed for a second by the sheer beauty of Jessi. Who'd have guessed that she would be a femme fatale without even trying? He fiddled with the strap on his overnight bag to distract himself.

But there was no distraction from Jessi. Her perfume danced on the wind and wrapped around his senses as he stood there in the eerie predawn light.

"Thanks for the lift," she said in that smart-ass way of hers that signaled the truce they'd sort of reached on the plane was over.

"You're welcome. It was an enjoyable flight," he said.

"Whatever. I figured I'd stay at Patti and John's bed-and-breakfast until we go home," she said.

"Fawkes has taken care of all the arrangements. The staff has canceled new arrivals, and when I spoke to the caretaker, he said there were only two couples left at the resort and that they would be leaving today."

"I guess that's one less thing to worry about," she said. "I'm more than ready to talk to their attorney and do whatever we need to do. Patti's mother isn't going to be much help…since she's ill."

Allan understood that Patti's mom, Amelia Pearson, was in the second stage of Alzheimer's-related dementia, but John had told him to keep it quiet, since Patti hadn't wanted anyone to know. He saw how thinking about Amelia's condition affected Jessi. Her shoulders were stooped for a second and he imagined it was from the burden of knowing that your best friend's own mother might not be able to mourn her.

"As soon as we see the attorney this morning we'll know more," he said. It wasn't something he was looking forward to, but at least Allan already knew a lot about John's wishes for the future. His friend had always been very loquacious and liked to share his dreams once he'd met and married Patti.

"I don't get why they wanted to live here," Jessi said. She glanced around the small airport. "I mean, it's nice enough to get away from the bustle of L.A. once in a while, but all the time? I don't think I could do it," she said. "It's going to take us over an hour to get to their place on Hatteras."

"I know, and my cell phone signal stinks. I think Kell is probably going to disown me if I don't check in, and I've only got one bar," Allan said.

Jessi pulled her iPhone out of her pocket and glanced

at the screen. "I've got almost two bars...want to use mine?"

He looked at her. As an olive branch gesture it was almost remarkable. She'd never offered him anything before. He tucked that fact away in the back of his mind to analyze later as he nodded at her.

"I have his number preprogrammed. He's listed under Darth Sucks-A-Lot," Jessi said as she handed the phone over.

Allan turned away to keep her from seeing the smile that spread across his face. He couldn't wait to tell Dec, who would think Jessi's tag for Kell was funny. "Don't let him see that. He hates *Star Wars*."

"Who hates *Star Wars*? Just another thing that proves your cousin is an alien cyborg," Jessi said. "Do you need privacy to talk to him?"

"Yes, if you don't mind."

"No problem. I'll go check with Fawkes about the car."

"Sounds good. Will you need to call your sisters?" he asked.

"Not at this time of the night. They both have little kids and will probably be sleeping," she said. "Are you sure Kell will be up at 4:00 a.m.?"

"Yes. He only needs four hours of sleep a night. Plus he'll be waiting for me to check in," Allan said.

"Of course, since he's some kind of future-engineered, high-performing robot," she said, walking away.

Allan watched her leave, as he had many times before, but now he noticed how her entire body moved. The swish of her hips in those skintight leather pants, the way the heels on her boots canted her hips forward and made her legs seem miles long. The way the tail of her blousy shirt curved around her ass.

He appreciated her as a woman, and despite how chaotic things were inside him right now, watching her walk was like a balm. It reminded him that he was still alive.

He hit the auto dial for Kell and waited three rings until his cousin picked up.

"Montrose here."

"It's Allan."

"What number are you calling me from?" he asked. "I had this down as someone else's."

"It's Jessi's phone. Mine isn't working right and I couldn't get a signal, but hers did. I wanted to check in and see if I missed anything last night."

"Not much. I sent you an email that details everything I need done today. Will you have reception later?" Kell asked.

Allan felt as if he had to defend the fact that the cell towers in this part of the world weren't thick on the ground. But he knew Kell wasn't irritated with him per se, but more with anything that interrupted the normal flow of business. "I don't know. John has Wi-Fi at his place so once I get there we should be good to go. I'm going to be busy this morning with the attorney and the funeral arrangements, but I'll get everything back to you today."

"That's what I was hoping you'd say. It's not much, but I need you to run some figures on a pro forma that Emma submitted. Also, I've talked to Dec, and unless Jessi pulls out something spectacular we're in favor of offering her a package and cutting her from the company. I need you to work on that today."

"Can't you cut me a little slack? I get that this is business, but we're dealing with the loss of our best friends," he said.

There was silence on the other end of the phone, and Allan wondered if he'd pushed Kell too far.

"You're right. I can give you both a few extra days. How are you holding up?"

"Fine," Allan said. "You know me."

"I do, which is why I don't buy that B.S. answer. You and John were like brothers."

"It's hard, Kell," Allan said. "But I can't talk about it."

"Fair enough. I'm here if you need me," he stated.

Allan knew that his older cousin would be there for him. Despite how cold he seemed in the office and how single-minded he could be in his quest for revenge against the Chandlers, Kell had a very strong sense of loyalty to both his cousins.

"I'll call when I know something more. I'm going to have to reboot my phone, so until I notify you, call me on this number."

He clicked off and thought about his cousin's hard-line attitude. Kell was determined to let Jessi go, and there was nothing Allan could do to save her. And a part of him was very glad about that, because she was the kind of complication he didn't need in his life for the long term, even though he knew that she was in it for the foreseeable future.

The Land Rover Fawkes had arranged for them to use was a new model. It was spacious and comfortable and had four-wheel drive, something that seemed important out here in the wilderness of North Carolina.

Fawkes had stowed their bags in the back of the vehicle and then opened the door to the backseat for Jessi. She stood for a minute as the warm breeze stirred around her. The sun was rising and for a minute she enjoyed the view of the sun coming up over the ocean instead of her normal view of it sinking down into it.

"Thanks," she said, climbing in.

"You're welcome, Ms. Jessi."

"You can just call me Jessi, you know."

"Very well," Fawkes said.

Allan didn't say anything as he got into the passenger seat in the front, which suited Jessi just fine. She put her earbuds in her ears and pretended to disappear. She loved the fact that it was acceptable by society to do so, even though a part of her felt a bit rude. But right now she couldn't talk to anyone.

She didn't want to talk to anyone. Being here made Patti's death more real. Jessi watched as they left the small barrier island where the airport was located and crossed the bridge to another small strip of land. The Outer Banks were really just tiny bits of land that barely kept the sea at bay.

Once again she pondered Patti's choice in making her home here on the edge of the wilderness. It was pretty, though, she thought, as the sun continued to rise over the ocean. They turned right at Whale Bone Junction Information Station and followed NC 12 south, crossing the Oregon Inlet Bridge. She took her earbuds out when Allan gestured toward her.

"Yes?"

"Seems like the end of the world, doesn't it?" he asked.

She nodded, a bit unnerved that they were thinking

along the same lines. Was it also occurring to him that if Patti and John hadn't moved out here maybe they'd still be alive?

"I think that's why Patti liked it," she said at last, unwilling to voice her real thoughts.

"I agree. No rat race here. Especially now that it's the off-season," Allan said. "Fawkes was just mentioning that the man at the desk in the airport warned him that that tropical storm in the Atlantic is now predicted to strengthen into a hurricane, and one of the projected paths has it coming straight toward Hatteras, where the B and B is located."

"Really?"

"Yes, ma'am—Jessi," Fawkes said. "I didn't think it would be a concern, but seeing these roads, I thought it best to mention it. Any kind of surge in the tide would wipe some of this out."

"I agree," Allan said. "Fawkes is going to keep an eye on the situation while we're taking care of the funerals and other arrangements. But if need be we should be ready for a quick escape."

"I always am," Jessi said.

"That's right, you are," he agreed. "So am I. But escaping a tricky personal situation and escaping Mother Nature are two different things."

She nodded. She put her earbuds back in as the conversation lagged. She was listening to Pink's latest and enjoying the mix of raw emotion and anger that Pink was always able to capture in her songs.

Twenty or so minutes into their drive, she noticed skid marks on the road. She pulled her earbuds from her ears as Fawkes slowed the Land Rover to a stop.

"Is this…?"

"I think so," Allan said, opening his door before Fawkes had the car in Park.

Jessi sat where she was, looking at the crushed grass, the wreckage from the other car and the remains of Patti's sweet little Miata, which still was there. Upside down and impossibly mangled.

Her heart started beating fast, and in her mind she heard screams. But she knew that was only her imagination. She got out of the vehicle and walked over to the side of the road. This was it, she thought.

Oh, God. This was it. This was how Patti and John had died, and it was worse than anything Jessi could have pictured in her head.

Car accident. Those words could mean anything, and the reality was so much harder to stomach than anything she'd imagined.

Staring at the wreckage, she heard the far-off sound of someone sobbing, and realized it was her. She turned away, not wanting Allan or even Fawkes to see her like this. But then she felt a hand on her shoulder.

When she turned back around, she didn't look up, but just moved forward, wrapping her arms around Allan's waist and burying her face in his chest. He held her tightly as she let loose the emotions she'd tried so unsuccessfully to tamp down.

She wanted to pretend that none of this had happened. But she had never been one for running away from the truth. And in this moment she knew she no longer could keep alive the very small hope that the authorities here had gotten it wrong. That Patti and John were still somehow alive.

No one had walked away from this scene. She knew it and accepted it. But the pain of losing her friend felt fresh and new, and so sharp that she couldn't breathe. Allan's hands moved up and down her back and she felt him shudder in her arms. Tipping her head back, she looked at the underside of his stubbled jaw.

When she noticed a thin line of tears running down his neck, she turned her head into the curve of his shoulder and held him as tightly as he held her.

She'd always seen him as her enemy. Even the ride out here and that kiss they'd shared on the plane hadn't really changed her perception—not at a gut-deep level. But in this moment, as she held on to the only other person in the world who understood her grief, she realized that he'd ceased being her rival.

Somehow in the past twenty-four hours he'd started to become simply Allan. Her Allan.

It was safe to assume he'd never felt this way before, and if he was completely honest, he never wanted to feel this way again. Losing John was making Allan question so many things, but most importantly, as he held Jessi in his arms, he wondered why he'd waited until his friend was gone to finally listen to him.

John had claimed from the beginning that he'd observed Allan and Jessi checking each other out when they thought no one was looking. And now, holding her in his arms, letting the tears he couldn't contain fall, Allan admitted that once again his friend had been right.

He felt a heavy hand on his shoulder and knew that Fawkes had joined them. The three of them, who'd never gotten along, were now united in grief.

And Allan had to wonder how much of what he felt at this moment was simply the need to feel the loss. The need to ensure that the empty part of his soul was filled with something…someone. He didn't want to be alone and didn't want to lose the memories he had of John, and whether he liked it or not…well, right now he'd be lying if he said he didn't like the fact that Jessi was here with him. She was the one he wanted to be with.

"I didn't think I'd fall apart like that," she said.

Pulling away, Fawkes walked closer to the wreckage, leaving the two of them alone. The breeze off the Atlantic was warm and strong, and for a minute Allan wished it could carry them away from here.

But that was only because he had no idea how to handle his grief. He turned his head away from Jessi and wiped his eyes before turning back.

"I saw you cry," she said, her tone kind and the look in her eyes one of the softest he'd ever seen. Her short punky hair was flying about in the wind, and her eye makeup had run from her tears, leaving dark tracks down her face.

"I saw *you* cry," he said, trying hard for a teasing note he just didn't feel.

"I guess we're even then," she said at last. "You know what?"

"What?" he asked. He wasn't sure he wanted to keep talking when every word she said made him feel raw and exposed.

"I'd be happy to lose to you now if it meant Patti and John were still here."

One of the things Allan had always respected about Jessi was her honesty, even when it would serve her better to lie. At first he'd thought her bluntness was just another tool she used to keep him disarmed, but then he'd realized that she had no barriers.

It had been his first clue that the girl who looked as if she'd take on hell with a bucket of water was actually vulnerable. He didn't need to be reminded of that right now. He needed her fierce and prickly, needed her to be his enemy. But he feared that ship had sailed. He was never going to look at Jessi the same way again.

"Me, too," he admitted.

"What the hell happened out here?" Jessi asked. "I know they were hit and then drove into the tree, but really, who would be driving that fast on this kind of road?"

"An idiot," Allan said. Inside, he felt some of that rage, as well. But his modus operandi was to channel it into graciousness and fake ennui. "I hope I never meet the guy," he added.

"Same here. I don't think it would be easy to have to see the person who caused this and… It would just be too much, you know?"

"I do know," he said as she looked up at him with that gaze of hers that cut through a man and made him feel he was completely exposed from the inside out. God, Allan hated that. He didn't want Jessi to see him—really see him.

She started laughing, and he glanced at her to see if she was okay or if she was truly losing it.

She shook her head. "Sorry. I was just thinking that we're finally getting along. Patti would be giving me an I-told-you-so look if she were alive at this moment."

"John would, too," Allan said. He couldn't count the number of times his buddy had taken him to one side and asked him to give Jessi a chance. To stop baiting Patti's best friend and just let her into that protected inner circle of trust that Allan fiercely guarded.

"Why didn't we?" she asked. "Why didn't we do this before they were gone? They were our dearest friends. All they wanted was for us to get along, and we could never be anything but enemies."

"We are 'enemies' because there's something very similar in both of us, and we were raised to distrust each other's families. We like to win, we like to protect our friends, and mostly, we don't like it when anyone notices that we aren't invincible," he said.

She crossed her arms over her chest, and then with a sigh uncrossed them and turned to face him. "I don't want to admit this, but there is a small kernel of truth in what you just said."

He felt the band of tension inside of him loosen.

"I was right?" he asked. Those were words he'd been positive that Jessi Chandler would never utter in his presence.

"Don't let it go to your head," she said, putting her arms around her waist and turning to walk back toward the Land Rover. "I'm pretty sure that it won't happen again."

For the first time since he'd gotten the awful news that John was dead, Allan felt something. He wanted to pretend it was lust, because just looking at Jessi made him want her. Or maybe he could explain it away as shared grief. But the truth of the matter was much harder to accept.

He liked her. He liked being with her. And he'd have to say, in all honesty, that he wanted this new feeling to grow.

Five

Jessi sat next to Allan in the attorney's office, trying to let the newest shock sink in.

Reggie Blythe was a tall, thin African American man who looked to be in his mid-fifties. He had a little gray at his temples and a wiry look that said he spent more time at work than at home. Jessi thought that his office had a charming Old South feel to it, but freely admitted to herself that the impression came from images she'd seen in Hollywood movies.

She felt nervous and unsure. She didn't know how to handle this meeting or Allan.

Actually, it was only Allan who was shaking her up right now. She could handle attorneys. But Allan was something else.

Reggie had been giving them a rundown on John and Patti's will and their hopes for Hannah's upbringing. But Jessi was busy looking at Allan and remembering that moment when they'd stopped by the accident scene and he'd held her in his arms. He had just offered comfort, and been so damned human that she'd had to rethink everything.

Not just what she'd thought about him, but also what she'd always believed about herself.

"I don't understand. Is that even legal?" Allan asked.

Damn. She needed to pay better attention. What had he said?

"It's highly unusual for joint custody to be given to two people who aren't married, but it's not illegal," Reggie said.

"Why would they do this?" Jessi asked. It was slowly sinking in that Patti and John had left custody of Hannah to her and Allan, even though they'd known that she and Allan didn't really like each other.

"I suspect they didn't anticipate dying so young," Reggie said with a wry note in his voice. "Also that they wanted to ensure Hannah had influences from both sides of her parents' lives."

"Of course. Where is Hannah now?" Allan asked.

"She's in state custody now. We couldn't keep her with her babysitter, but we'll be turning her over to you both as soon as this meeting is finished," Reggie said, glancing at his watch.

"And that's it? We can just go back to L.A.?" Jessi asked.

"No. A judge will be reviewing the case, and once you are both approved as joint guardians, then you can return to California. Patti and John have already paid me to serve as your legal counsel in the proceedings, unless you have objections and would like your own attorney."

"What if one of us isn't interested in being a guardian?" Allan asked.

"Is that the case?" Reggie asked, his kind brown eyes meeting Allan's gaze first before shifting to Jessi.

Allan didn't say anything else. Jessi was worried. She knew nothing about raising a baby—in fact, she'd already decided she wasn't ever having kids. But this was Patti's final request, and she found that she couldn't deny her friend.

"Can we have a moment alone to discuss this?" Jessi asked.

"Of course. You may use my office," he said, getting up to leave the room. When the door closed behind him she turned to Allan.

He stood and paced to the window, pausing with the sun behind him, which made it very difficult for her to see his expression. He didn't seem like the Allan who'd held her so tenderly and shared her grief. He seemed like the old Allan, maneuvering around while trying to figure out the best position to be in.

She didn't like it. Which man was the real one? She wanted him to be…something she suspected he couldn't be. But maybe she should give him the benefit of the doubt. He was in the same situation she was. Just as blown away by the fact that they were going to be raising a little girl.

Or were they? Would he stand by her and help her or was she going to be doing this on her own?

"Do you not want to be a guardian?" she asked bluntly.

"Of course I do. She's John's daughter and he was closer to me than a brother. I only voiced that option in case you wanted an out but were too timid to ask," he said.

"Are you kidding me? I don't do timid," she said. "You know that. So what's this all about?"

Allan walked toward her. As he moved closer, she

could see for the first time since she'd met him a very sincere look on his face. He wasn't doing the fake charming thing or acting as if he could buy his way out of this.

"I don't walk away from commitments," he said. "John and Patti must have had their reasons for appointing both of us. I don't know what they were, but today I started to see a glimpse of it. I'm just not sure if you did."

"I did," she admitted. "But is this real?"

"We won't know until we get Hannah and return to the West Coast."

"I agree. I can't say no to this," Jessi said.

"Me, either."

The atmosphere in the room was becoming too heavy, the situation too real, and she didn't like it. She needed time to process the fact that Allan was going to be in her life for the rest of it. She started doing the logistics. "So what are we going to do?" she asked. "I mean, from a practical standpoint. I live in Malibu."

"I'm in Beverly Hills," Allan said.

"Well, we can hand her off to each other at work," Jessi said. "I'm not as familiar with the Playtone Games campus, but if we use the facility at Infinity, they have a first-rate day care center where Hannah can stay during our working hours. Then we can divide up her nights."

"I like that plan, but we should have a contingency in case your probation doesn't work out," Allan said.

She made a face at him. Of course he'd bring that up. "I'm not going to lose my job. I've already told you I have some new ideas."

"I'm just saying we should figure out some more options," he said. "I like to plan for every eventuality."

She wondered if she'd ever really know what he was thinking. Then she shook her head. She had other things to worry about than that. Hannah, her future, dealing with Allan every day from now on. It was a big responsibility and one Jessi wouldn't shirk. She'd figure out a way to make this work.

"I guess it's decided then," she said.

"Yes, I'll go and get Reggie."

She sat back in the leather chair and tried to relax, but she couldn't. Every time she thought she'd adjusted to losing Patti there was something new that surprised her. Jessi ran her hands through her short hair and realized it was getting easier to think about her friend being gone. Not *easier;* that wasn't the right word. She just could do it without crying, which was a relief.

She'd always hated the fact that she couldn't control her tears. In general, she didn't cry unless she was mad, but this kind of grief, well, she supposed there was only one way for it to be expressed.

She heard the door open and turned to see Allan striding in with Reggie. Allan was a bit taller than the attorney and had his head bent to listen intently to what Reggie was saying. For all the world they looked as if they'd known each other for years. Typical of Allan, she thought. The man never met a stranger.

"Allan has told me the good news that you both will share guardianship. I can't tell you how happy that would have made Patti and John. They were adamant that they wanted their best friends to raise their daughter," Reggie said.

"Well, we really want to honor their wishes," Jessi answered.

"Good. I've got some paperwork for you to fill out,

and then I'll drive you over to get Hannah. The authority from the state wants to check you both out and ask you a few questions before she's released to you temporarily. I've already got a call in to the judge's office for scheduling."

"How long do you think this entire process will take?" Allan asked. "I'm— We're both needed back in L.A."

"I don't think it will take too long—maybe a week to ten days."

A week was definitely too long to Jessi's way of thinking. Hell, the plane flight with Allan had seemed endless. Sure, she knew there was no speeding this type of thing up, and there shouldn't be. She wanted the state officials to do their job and ensure that Hannah was going to be well cared for.

But staying in Hatteras with the man who was turning out to be her Achilles' heel didn't sound ideal. And she needed to think of the future. When it was just her it wouldn't have mattered if she lost her job at Playtone-Infinity Games. But now that she was going to be an example to Hannah...

Dammit, Jessi was going to have to rethink everything she'd thought she knew about herself, and reorder her priorities for Hannah's sake.

And that meant trying to get along with Mr. Allan McKinney, not liking him more than she already did, and most importantly, staying out of his bed.

When Reggie drove them to the foster home where Hannah was being kept, Jessi realized she was glad they'd gotten to Hatteras when they did. The home was nice enough from the outside, but the people inside were strangers to the baby girl. The sooner she was set up in a more permanent custody arrangement, the better.

"Hi there, I'm Di, and this my husband, Mick. We own a local restaurant and knew John and Patti," the foster mother said as they entered the house.

"This is Allan McKinney and Jessi Chandler, Hannah's guardians," Reggie replied.

"I'll go get her," Di said, as Mick led them into the living room.

Jessi was too nervous to really pay attention to the conversation. Inside, she was a quivering mess, because she knew next to nothing about babies. She always avoided holding her sisters' kids because she was afraid of dropping them or breaking them in some way. And she hadn't held Hannah for more than five minutes in her short life. Jessi figured she didn't have a maternal bone in her body. "Here she is," Di said, returning with a sleepy-looking Hannah.

Jessi went over and held her arms out, and Di handed her the baby. Jessi felt awkward and unsure until she looked down into those eyes that were so similar to Patti's.

This was Patti's daughter, Jessi thought. She held her closer and had a moment's horror as she realized she was about to start crying. She tried to turn away, but then Allan was there by her side. He didn't say anything, just wrapped his arm around her and looked over her shoulder at the baby.

Jessi didn't feel as overwhelmed when he was touching her. She wasn't alone. It didn't matter that there were still big issues between the two of them; they were united in this and right now that was all that mattered.

"I guess John and Patti's instincts were correct,"

Reggie said. "You two are going to make good guardians of their little girl."

"We will do our best," Allan said, looking Jessi straight in the eye.

It felt as if he was making a promise to her, and she couldn't help but feel as if together they would make this work. But she wondered how her sisters and his cousins would react to the news that she and Allan were going to be raising a child together.

She felt a twinge as she imagined the look on Darth-Sucks-A-Lot's face when he heard that another one of his cousins was so closely involved with a Chandler sister. But that little bit of mirth didn't change the fact that she and Allan were going to have to figure out how to be friends, because they were going to be the closest thing to parents that Hannah had.

"We can't screw this up," Jessi said.

"We won't," Allan answered. "We both are very good at making things happen the way we want them to."

Allan poured himself two fingers of Scotch and put his feet up on the railing as the sun set over Pamlico Sound. He was making promises he had no business making, he thought. But being here in John's old home, he found it hard not to feel the man he was in L.A. slipping away. The water was still and calm, and there was a soothing element to sitting here and forgetting about the long forty-eight hours he'd just lived through. Today had seemed endless, and he was more than ready for it to be over.

They'd finished making the funeral arrangements. In the end it had made more sense to have a joint ceremony, and Jessi had been very efficient at managing the little details.

Seeing that side of her had made him realize why she was so good at her job. He'd seen the reports on the interviews that Dec had conducted with the employees at Infinity Games. They'd all said that Jessi was singularly organized and always successfully launched their games.

Allan rubbed the back of his neck. He was square in the middle of it right now. Kell's hatred… Was it really just Kell who resented the Chandlers anymore? Allan knew that he'd started out with just as much anger toward them, but right now it was hard not to see the Chandlers, especially Jessi, as real people.

People who weren't part of the long-ago feud.

Jessi had volunteered to give little Hannah a bath after dinner, and he'd let her. He knew that she was tired, too, and maybe he should have been gentlemanly and stepped in to do it, but he wasn't ready to deal with a child yet.

He decided to text his cousin Dec, who was the father of a toddler himself. Of course, Dec had just met his son for the first time a few months earlier, but that made his perspective perfect for Allan. He needed some info, and quick, if he was going to do what he always did—make life look effortless. Because the baby was already throwing him off.

She'd cried and then spit up on his shirt, and he hadn't been too successful at diaper changing, either. He'd have to fix this situation. He didn't allow anything to get the better of him and he certainly didn't intend to start now.

He'd managed to reboot his phone so that he had cell coverage now. He messaged Dec.

Help. How do you deal with a baby?

The phone immediately rang and he answered it. "McKinney here."

"I love it. The great Allan McKinney doesn't know what to do," Dec said.

"I doubt you knew what to do the first time you held D.J."

"True. I didn't. Do you want me to ask Cari for advice?"

"No. Don't you dare. Just wanted to know how you handled it when you met D.J."

"I was afraid I'd break him. I kind of held him at arm's length. But then after I started spending time with him, I realized two things—one, it didn't matter what I said if I talked in a quiet, kind tone, and two, everyone screws up with kids. Even Cari, though she'll deny it."

"Thanks for that. Hannah's a little girl, Dec. I don't know anything about girls. I mean, we were all boys...."

Dec laughed. "You seem to do okay with women."

"Hannah's not a woman. This is different. I can't be charming or do all the things I know women expect a man to do. I have to be—"

"Real," Dec said. "It's that way with D.J. for me. I can't just phone it in. Kids require more. Hannah's a baby, and she's new to this situation just like you are. You'll figure it out."

"I hope so. I've downloaded a few books about child rearing on my Kindle app. But I needed to talk to someone who's actually done this."

"Well, that's all I got without asking my woman," Dec said.

"I'd rather you didn't, since she'd probably tell her sister," Allan said.

"How's that situation?"

He had no idea how to answer his cousin. The truth was, Jessi irritated him more now than she had two days ago. But she also fascinated him more. And he was obsessed with her, spending his time thinking about how soft her skin was and how much he liked her perfume.

Finally, he just said, "Good. We're both making the best of it. The funeral is going to be in four days' time. Are you coming? I can send the jet back for you."

"Yes. That would be great. I know that Cari and Emma are both interested in attending. Kell doesn't want to travel with them. In fact, he said he might not come at all."

"I'm worried about him. He has too much hatred toward the Chandlers," Allan said.

"Me, too. But what can we do? Hey, do you want to go with me when the Lakers play the Mavs in two weeks? Cari has to work," Dec asked.

Allan smiled to himself. He and Dec had grown closer since Dec had come back from Australia and found himself a family.

"Love to. Later, dude."

"Later," Dec said, disconnecting the call.

Allan skimmed the first book he'd downloaded on his phone, and felt a lot better about the next few days than he had before. After a while, he put his Scotch aside and got up to go find Jessi.

He wasn't too confident that their child-sharing plan was going to be successful. Even though Hannah was tiny she seemed to require a lot of attention, and two heads were better than one.

He wondered… Should he suggest that the three of them live together? It might cause less disruption for Hannah and help them both out. But he didn't know if his self-control was up to having Jessi in the same house. Already just the thought of her sleeping down the hall was enough to make him contemplate things he knew he shouldn't.

He heard the sound of singing and went to investigate. As he got closer, he realized that Jessi was singing Pink's "Blow Me" to Hannah as she dressed the baby.

Not exactly Brahms, he thought as he stood in the door of the nursery. But he saw that Hannah seemed to like it; she was slapping her hands and staring up at Jessi.

When Jessi finished singing the song, she said, "That was Pink. Your mom and I saw her in concert about eight times. For a while we both had our hair cut real short like Pink's. And your mom…"

All of a sudden Jessi's voice broke and she leaned in close, lifting Hannah off the changing table and into her arms, burying her head on top of the baby's. Allan started to back away. This moment was between the two of them, and he knew he'd be intruding.

Suddenly, that song seemed entirely right for her to sing to the baby. It was something that Patti and Jessi had shared. This was why their friends had named them coguardians. So that their daughter would never forget either one of them.

It also underscored why Jessi and Allan couldn't live together, ever. The more times he saw her looking like a real woman—not a punk pain-in-his-ass, but a real human being—the harder it would be for him to help Kell fire her.

And he knew that he was going to have to do that. His cousin had better appreciate the situation that Allan was in right now. It was hard enough to fire someone he knew casually. But to do it to a woman he was starting to like and respect and—ah, hell—really care for… There was no way he was going to be able to do it and not lose a little part of himself.

Six

Jessi had thought everything was going well with Hannah until she and Allan were watching *The Daily Show* and the baby started crying. Jessi tried to comfort the little girl, but nothing seemed to work. Singing had calmed Hannah down earlier, but no way was she going to sing in front of Allan.

"Your turn," she said, picking the baby up and taking her over to Allan.

"Gladly. Why don't you go and get yourself a drink?" he suggested.

Though she'd been planning to do just that, she decided not to. She didn't want to let the dynamic between the two of them change now. It would be too easy to fall into the pattern of roommates…and much more. And she'd already promised herself that what had happened on the flight out here wouldn't happen again.

Kissing him had been a mistake, and given that they were now alone together, with Fawkes mostly out of the way in the guest quarters, she had to be especially careful to keep her sexual urges firmly under control. But even though she had about a million other things on her mind, the images of kissing Allan kept cropping up.

Right now she hoped that Hannah would settle down and go to sleep early, because tomorrow they had a lot of stuff to do, including going to visit Hannah's grandmother. It was a visit that Jessi wasn't looking forward to, but she knew it had to be done.

She had talked privately to Reggie Blythe and knew that the care home had been notified of Patti's death. But Jessi wouldn't feel right unless she went and visited Amelia herself.

She noticed that Allan was walking around the room with Hannah. The little girl had her binky in her mouth and was now sleeping. Jessi told herself it was just beginner's luck, but a part of her was jealous that he'd been able to get the baby to sleep when she hadn't.

"I'll go put her down," he said in a very quiet voice.

She nodded.

As soon as he left the room she stretched her legs out on the couch, put her head back against the armrest and stared at the ceiling. They were in the back of the bed-and-breakfast in the suite of rooms that John and Patti had lived in. It was small compared to her place in Malibu, but so homey. Everywhere Jessi looked she saw her friend's touch, and it made her miss Patti that much more.

She rubbed her forehead, thinking that she'd better get started on a decent marketing plan tonight. She'd already had one email from Kell telling her that her deadlines for delivering her items hadn't been changed.

She felt torn. It went against her nature to back down, but this time she just didn't feel like the fight was worth it. Even Allan, who didn't hate her as much as Kell did, had intimated that she was probably not going to be keeping her role at the end of her probationary period. Should she put in the effort?

It was just one more thing she had to contemplate. A part of her liked the thought of her, Allan and Hannah all spending the day in the same place. And that made Jessi contemplate a future for herself that she'd never wanted. For a minute she felt like a little girl. The little girl she'd been before reality had intruded and taught her that things like perfect families didn't happen all the time the way they did in TV sitcoms.

She was okay with that. She prided herself on being a realist, but now that she'd had a glimpse of domesticity she'd be lying if she said she didn't want it for herself. A part of her did want to be part of a family unit.

But that was a pipe dream, probably brought on by Patti's death. Hell, it wasn't even Jessi's dream. She'd never wanted a husband to tell her what to do, the way her father had dominated her mother's life and her choices. Never wanted a child who could be used as a pawn in that relationship.

She sat up and leaned forward, putting her elbows on her knees. She had to fight for her job at the newly merged Playtone-Infinity Games. And then she had to do her best to raise Hannah to be strong, but also open to love, the way Patti had been. Jessi sensed that had been why her friend had wanted her to be coguardian. Because Allan would never let the little girl want for anything material. But there were things a man—a father—wouldn't understand about a daughter.

"Are you sure you don't want a drink? I'm getting myself one," Allan said from the doorway. He'd changed out of his suit and had on a pair of basketball shorts that rode low on his hips and a loose-fitting Lakers tank top.

She couldn't speak as she stared at his chest. He was lean and tan—not like some gym-crazed guy, just fit. Damn, she didn't need a reminder of just how good-looking he was. Or how much she still wanted him.

She had to ignore her baser instincts....

"Do you want a drink?" he repeated.

"Yes, please," she said at last, and then realized it had to have been obvious to him that she'd been staring at him. "Are you getting them?"

"I was planning on it," Allan said.

"I wasn't sure you could function without your butler, and since Fawkes is staying in the guest quarters..."

"I think I can manage to get us both a beer. Then I'm hoping to catch a little of the Lakers game," he said. "Want to watch it with me?"

"Yes, but I have work to do. And you mentioned giving me some contacts," she said.

"I believe our contest ended in a draw."

"It did. But Kell isn't budging on his deadlines and I could really use some help."

"I'll email the information over to you," he said. "But I'd rather you stay and watch the game with me."

"Why?" she asked. "I know you don't think I can pull it off, but I'm intent on saving my job."

"I'm sure you'll do it. I've seen you in action before. But for tonight I'd rather just enjoy some time with the one person who must feel the emptiness in this room as keenly as I do."

Jessi swallowed hard, surprised he'd mentioned what they'd both been avoiding: that without John and Patti, being here felt wrong somehow.

* * *

"I've got an idea," Allan said as he came back into the room with two beers.

"For what?"

"To distract us," he said.

"We need distracting?"

"I do, Jess. I'm on the edge here and I don't like it."

"What don't you like?" she asked, in that way of hers that made him want to just bare his soul and stop pretending that he wasn't attracted to her.

No matter what had happened in the past two days, she'd made adjustments and seemed to be dealing with everything okay. And he wanted to know how she did it. On the outside, sure, he looked like a guy who was holding it together, but on the inside…he was a hot mess. And he hated that.

Emotions made a man sloppy, and made Allan in particular realize how often he'd pushed them aside to keep focused on the path ahead. But being here in John's living room with his baby sleeping down the hall, and knowing that he was going to be raising her with this woman had shaken him to his core.

"Emotions," he admitted. "I need something to take my mind off things."

"And the basketball game can't do that?"

"Not when you are sitting there looking sexy," he said.

"I look sexy?" she asked. "I'm wearing a button-down shirt and a denim skirt. Not exactly femme fatale gear."

"It is on you," he said. "All evening long I've been sitting here watching you and thinking about that kiss on the plane. The one we both meant to be a competition that turned into something else entirely."

Suddenly, she didn't look smug or aloof. She looked intrigued and vulnerable. The way he felt inside.

"So what's your solution?"

"The way I see it," he said, moving into the room and handing her the beer he'd poured for her, "we've got two choices."

"Two?" she asked, and he noticed that when he sat down right next to her on the couch, she didn't scoot over. In fact, she sort of leaned a little bit toward him.

He nodded and took a sip of his beer before he said, "We could always ignore this and hope that it goes away. But to be honest, I'm not that good at ignoring a beautiful woman."

"Don't lie to me," she said.

"I'm not."

"Really? I know I'm not beautiful," she declared. "I'm cute and sexy, but beautiful—not so much."

"We'll have to agree to disagree on this," he said. He didn't know how she defined beauty, but for him she was the embodiment of everything female. She was strong enough to know who she was, bold enough to go after what she wanted, and also smart enough to admit when she needed someone. Earlier, she'd needed him, and that had awakened something inside Allan that he didn't know how to control.

"You were saying?"

"We can either ignore the attraction between us or face it, decide to have an affair and see where it leads," he said.

"Are you trying to shock me?" she asked.

"Nah, I do say things sometimes to throw you off.

Mainly to see if you react. But seriously, those are our only choices, ya know?"

"Ignoring it doesn't seem like it's going to work," she said slowly. "Right now you are the only person I can turn to. And I haven't been able to stop thinking about that kiss, either."

"What have you been thinking?" he asked.

She tipped her head to the side and took a slow sip of her beer. "Are you sure you want me to be honest?"

"Hell, yeah. I'm laying it all on the line here," he said.

"I liked it better when you were just my enemy…that douche, Allan. I don't want to think of you as the guy who makes me hot and wet."

Her words were evocative and made him harden in his pants. He wanted to say screw it, then take her hand and lead her to the bedroom. But what he wanted was physical, not emotional.

Liar, he thought. But he really wanted to keep the two things separate if he could.

And he wanted to keep her hot and wet.

"You said be honest," she said. "Did I shock you?"

"A little, but I shouldn't be. You've never been shy about speaking your mind."

"True. Plus I wanted to see if you were as horny as I am."

"Stop. We can't have a logical discussion if you keep talking like that."

"Why not?"

"Keep pushing me, Jessi, and I'll prove to you that you've barely seen hot and wet."

"I'm tempted to," she said.

"Why?"

"If I keep pushing and you react, then neither of us is responsible. We can blame hormones."

"But neither of us would believe that," he said, watching as she took another delicate sip of her beer.

She tossed her head and then leaned forward to set her glass on the coffee table. "I'm tempted, Allan. But I can't do it. Emma would kill me if I hooked up with you and screwed up something at Infinity for her."

"This has nothing to do with our families."

"Sure, we can say that now, but we both know it would impact them," she said. "Emma is already struggling, and with Dec and Cari…it just makes things difficult at times."

Allan understood what she meant. Kell was difficult. He still hated the Chandlers. Allan had been trying to stay neutral as Dec tried to influence them to go easier on the Chandler sisters.

"So we're still at a crossroads," he said. He'd always been very good at reading people, but Jessi had never been easy for him. Yet he had a hunch that giving in to the attraction might be a solution for them. But it would mean mixing together the two separate areas of his life, something he'd never done before. And it would mean showing Jessi a part of himself he preferred to keep private. Yet at the same time it could be the answer to this entire sexual tension thing that was going on between them.

"I'm okay with ignoring it until we get back from North Carolina, but I don't know how successful I'll be. I'm not handling Patti's death as well as I wish I was. I can't be philosophical about it."

"I'm not handling it well, either," he said, still searching for the words that would give them both what they needed. "That's why I brought this up."

He put his free hand on the back of the sofa and touched the skin at the base of her neck. Jessi flinched, spilling some of her beer on him. Her eyes were glassy and he didn't have to be Sherlock Holmes to guess that thinking of Patti was going to make her cry.

"Sorry about that," she said.

"Sorry is not enough," he said.

"It's not? That was just a drop of beer."

He arched one eyebrow at her. And she reached for his thigh, rubbing her finger over the spot the beer had left.

"What do you think I should do about it?" she asked.

"Clean it up," he said.

She leaned back and crossed her arms over her chest. "You surprise me, Allan. You know I'm not the type of woman to take orders from a man."

He shouldn't be surprised. Jessi had been making him uncomfortable since they met. Unlike most of the women he dealt with, she hadn't been wowed by his charm or money. He'd put that down to their family rivalry, but it was more than that.

"There is a lot about me you don't know," he said at last. "And I think there's a lot about you I haven't seen yet, either. I'm willing to bet that you take orders when it suits you."

"Maybe. It depends on the man," she said in that quiet way of hers, watching him with that gaze that was almost too serious. She shook her head and he thought that would be the end of it.

"I'm the right man," he said. "And I'm waiting."

* * *

Jessi hated to admit it, but she was intrigued. He was flirting around with something that had always been a secret fantasy of hers. She was so bold in life that most men expected her to be the aggressor once they got to the bedroom. But Allan didn't.

She wondered if she could actually do it, even though the thought of giving over control of her body to a man had always been a turn-on. She wasn't sure that giving up control to Allan was something she could embrace, but she'd always been a never-say-never type girl. "I don't know. I'm leaning more toward just handing you a towel and letting you dry your shorts," she said.

He shrugged, and she watched his body movements with different eyes now. What did it say about the out-wardly effusive man that he liked his sex controlled and with limits? She didn't want to know. Really, she didn't. She liked keeping Allan in the jerk category. It made life easier when he didn't seem multidimensional. She could just not like him and move on.

But now…now he was starting to seem human and real to her. She groaned.

"What?" he asked. "What are you afraid of?"

"Not you," she said hastily, and then realized she probably had given away the fact that he did unnerve her. "I don't want to make things awkward between us."

"When hasn't it been?" he asked. "Listen, we're at-tracted to each other whether we like it or not. Our lives are forcing us to be with each other. So we can either let this thing control us or—"

"We can control it," she said. She leaned back on the cushions of the couch and looked at him. Taking her time and letting her gaze start at his feet and move slowly up to his waist and his chest, to his face.

He was good-looking but he wasn't classically handsome. Though there was something in the blunt cut of his lips that made it hard for her not to lick her own at the thought of his mouth against hers again.

He sat there, all arrogant male, and then did the one thing that tipped things in his favor. He held his hand out to her.

He hesitated for a second and then closed the gap between them. He took the back of her head in his hand, his grip on her firm but not forceful, and brought his mouth down hard on hers.

If their last kiss was exploratory and new, this one was about domination, and left no doubts in her. He wanted her. She knew that whether she wanted to admit it or not, she was going to end up in Allan's bed.

Allan McKinney. *Dammit,* she thought. *Why him?* Why did he have to be the man to make her feel like this?

But then she stopped thinking as his mouth moved over hers. His tongue plunged deep inside and she shifted, trying to get closer to him. She opened her mouth wider and sucked on his tongue, but that still didn't bring the relief she sought. She tried to lean in closer to him. Wanted to feel his body wrapped around hers, but he lifted his head and eased away from her.

His lips were swollen and wet from kissing her, his face flushed with desire. His silver eyes narrowed as his kept his gaze fixed on her, and she shivered with awareness, but also anticipation.

She did want what he was offering. The attraction to him was more powerful than she wanted it to be, but she wasn't about to lie to herself. It existed and she wasn't going to be happy until she had him in her bed.

She leaned toward him, but he held up a hand to stop her. "No. That was just a sample of what I can offer you, but there is no halfway. If you want this take my hand."

She wasn't entirely clear what he was offering, but at this point, with her pulse racing and every nerve in her body crying out for more, she really wasn't going to turn away. If one kiss could do that to her…she had to find out what else was in store.

It had been too long since she'd had really good sex. The trouble with the takeover and her general dissatisfaction with her career had conspired to keep her from focusing on her needs. And now Allan was offering her a solution to that situation.

She lifted her hand and saw how small it looked when he clasped it in his. His nails were square and blunt, his fingers large, his palm warm. There was strength and control in his grasp.

She nibbled at her bottom lip as he drew her close, until barely an inch of space separated them. He put his forefinger under her chin and tipped her head back, making her look up at him. He didn't say anything, just let his gaze move over her face.

She noticed he paused as he took in the small diamond in the side of her nose, and then his hand moved down her neck to trace the pattern of her tattoo. The small raven was her reminder not to let herself be swept away, and for the first time since she'd made the decision to get the tattoo, at age eighteen, she realized she was in very real danger of not heeding its warning.

Seven

Jessi felt small under his hands. He used his touch on her back to turn her and draw her toward him.

Seeming eager for his kiss, she lifted her face toward his, so he nipped her lower lip. Her tongue darted out and tangled with his, and he hardened.

He pulled her onto his lap. He took her hands and held them loosely behind her back, in the grip of one of his. She raised an eyebrow at him.

"We can't both be in control," he said.

"Why not?"

"That's not how I like things," he said. Then he brought his free hand up between them and ran his finger down the length of her neck. He liked touching her. Her skin was soft and the scent of it…peaches on a summer day.

"This doesn't work for me," she said. "I want to touch you. I don't want to be at your mercy."

"You already are," he said with confidence. She wasn't trying to get her hands free. She was sitting there waiting to see what he'd do next. He reached for the tasseled gold cord holding the decorative curtain in place and used it to bind her hands together behind her back. The cord was thick and didn't have much give. When he was done tying it, he reached for the buttons that ran down the front of her shirt.

She watched him with an unreadable gaze, but her breathing became more rapid, pushing her breasts against the fabric of her shirt. As the cloth fell away to reveal her cleavage, he paused to take a deep breath and admire her.

She was small but not tiny, her breasts full and suited to her frame. She wore a plain cotton bra, which surprised him. For a minute he'd expected a corset or something else punk. But he realized that the inner woman was very different from the outer one.

He ran his finger along the top curve of her breasts. "Do you like this?"

She shrugged, which pushed her breasts forward, and he reached beneath the fabric of her bra to caress one nipple. "It's different. There is something tantalizing about watching your reaction to my body."

"What do you see?"

"That you like touching me," she said. "You also like just looking at me. When you think I'm not watching, your eyes narrow and you stare at my breasts. What are you thinking?"

"I'm wondering what you'll look like naked."

"Why not find out?" she asked.

"I intend to, but in my own time," he said. Caressing her narrow waist, he ran his finger around her belly button. She shivered, and her stomach clenched. She liked being touched as much as he needed to touch her.

He reached behind her and undid the clasp of her bra and then pulled the straps forward on her arms until the fabric fell away, framing her breasts. Her nipples were a rosy-pink color and he cupped both breasts in his hands, rubbing his palm over them until they were hard. He leaned in to delicately lick at first one and then the other.

Jessi's hips moved against his erection, and he shifted his legs to get into a more comfortable position.

"Untie me," she said.

"Are you uncomfortable?" he asked.

"No," she said. "But my shirt is open…."

"I will untie you if you insist, but I like you this way and I think you do, as well," he said.

He leaned down to capture one nipple in his mouth. He suckled her and ran his tongue around it before biting lightly. "I like you this way!" he repeated

"I'm still deciding if I like you or not," she said.

Inside, he smiled. He wasn't too sure how much longer he could wait, but the knife's edge of anticipation made him feel…alive. And he knew that he'd keep this going for as long as he could.

He dipped his finger into his beer and rubbed it against her nipple, watching it tighten, before licking her slowly and then moving up her chest to taste her mouth with long, slow kisses. The saltiness of the beer and the taste of Jessi blended together, and he felt something clench deep inside him.

He was about to give in to the desire, free himself and take her. He knew it was time, knew he was hanging on to control by a thread. So he reached behind her to undo her hands and then set her next to him on the couch, tipping his head back to stare at the ceiling.

Jessi had never felt so sexually charged or as unnerved as she did at this moment. And she didn't like it. In fact, she'd rather just have a quickie than this.

The true problem was that it felt as if he was playing mind games. Her body was so turned on, but Allan was just sitting there, looking cool as could be. It was like their kiss on the airplane. A test to see who could hide their reactions the longest.

Right now she felt like the loser. Except...well not entirely. "I'm not sure this is the wisest bargain I've ever entered into with you."

He gave her one of his wry, knowing looks, and she shivered a little as she realized that he wasn't as unaffected as he wanted to be by their exchange.

"Nothing involving the opposite sex ever is," he said.

"Is that your motto?"

"No, actually, it was Grandfather's. But I have to admit the old bastard was right."

"What was he like?" Jessi asked to distract herself. She didn't really know that much about old Thomas Montrose. Unlike Allan and his cousins, who'd been taught to see the Chandlers as the enemy, she and her sisters hadn't really been raised to hate the Montrose family. As a matter of fact, a portrait of old Thomas had hung in the lobby of Infinity Games for as long as she could remember.

"He was bitter and thought only of revenge. That kind of attitude really taints a man's perspective."

"Yours?" she asked. As they talked, she almost forgot that her shirt was unbuttoned and her breasts were exposed, that there was nothing normal about the conversation they were having.

"No, Kell's. I don't think he's ever going to accept Cari as part of the merged company, and he really doesn't want you or Emma to come on board."

"What about you?" she asked.

"I'd rather buy you out, as well. But it's really hard to think about that stuff when you're sitting here like this," he admitted.

She breathed a little easier at his admission. "For me, too. But I'm sort of getting used to it."

"You are?"

"Now that I know it's distracting you," she said with a smile. Patti had always said there was more to Allan than the antagonist she knew.

"Still feel like backing down?" he asked.

"Never. I'm wondering if you are interested in me or if this is all a game to you?"

He stood up and took her wrist, drawing her hand to his crotch. "What do you think?"

She ran her palm over the heavy ridge of his erection. She stroked him through his shorts, wondering what he'd feel like naked in her grip. She used her forefinger to trace the line of his erection and heard his quick intake of breath.

She took hold of the waistband of his shorts and tugged it down slightly. But then stopped.

"What are you waiting for?" he asked.

"I thought you liked taking things slow," she said.

"Only if you are under me...taking me," he answered. She felt herself moisten and realized that this had long ago ceased being a game. Allan was the one man who could make her feel this way right now. She wasn't entirely sure she liked it, but she knew she wasn't going to walk away from him.

Their lives were entwined now and it was silly to pretend that they weren't.

"That doesn't sound like it's completely by the rules," she said.

"Nothing with you ever is," he said, picking her up in his arms and walking toward the bedroom at the back of the house.

She wrapped her arm around his shoulders and studied his face as he moved. There was a flush to his skin, which she put down to desire. There was a birthmark behind his left ear that she'd never noticed before. She traced the small kidney-shaped mark with her finger and he shivered and turned to face her, his silver eyes intense and sexual.

He definitely wasn't in the mood for games now and she was glad. She'd never been the kind of woman who liked to play around in the bedroom. She tried very hard not to equate sex with emotion, and instead tried in her own way to keep the two things separate, since she'd learned early in her dating life that most men did that.

"I like the way your hands feel on me," he said.

"Good, because I plan to put them all over you," she said.

He set her down on her feet next to the bed, put the baby monitor on the dresser and nudged the door closed with his hip. He kept his hands on her waist and they both just stood there for a long moment. In her mind this was the quiet before the storm. The moment when they both waited to see who would break first.

He lifted his hand and she felt his touch on her tattoo once again. He traced the shape of the raven over and over, and she felt shivers of intense pleasure move down her body from that one point of contact. She stood there watching the intensity on his face as he touched her.

It would be impossible to ever believe after this moment that she left him unaffected. She saw the proof of how much she turned him on in the narrowing of his eyes as he lowered his head toward hers, then felt it in the heat of his kiss.

His mouth moved over hers with surety and strength. He claimed her in that kiss. This was not the same way he'd teased and tempted from the first moment that they'd met. Now he was intent on leaving his mark on her, and as she reached for him and tried to draw their bodies together, she admitted to herself that she wanted nothing more than this.

For this moment it was enough to have him physically. She understood this wasn't her wisest decision and that there would be consequences, but she just didn't care.

She wanted him and she was determined to have him. She sucked his tongue deeper into her mouth, and as he held her by the waist with one hand to keep her from brushing her aching breasts against his chest, she reached between their bodies and stroked his erection.

His other hand moved from her neck, tracing a path straight down her ribs to her belly button. She'd had it pierced a few years ago, but had let the hole close up. Feeling the way he toyed with her navel made her wish she still had the piercing. His touch seemed too knowing and too intense for her, and she shifted a little, pulling her head back to look at him.

His eyes were half-closed, but she still felt the intensity of his gaze. He pushed her backward until her thighs hit the edge of the bed, and she sat down. He smiled at her as he pushed her shirt down her shoulders and off. She shrugged out of her bra and reached for his shorts. She didn't want to be the only one exposed.

She felt vulnerable and needed to keep the scales balanced between the two of them. If it had been any other man she would have changed positions, pushed him down on the bed and taken control. But with Allan everything was different—and it always had been.

In a moment of clarity, she admitted that from the first moment they'd met she'd felt a zing of attraction.

He grasped her hands to keep her from taking off his shorts. "Not yet."

"Yes," she said.

"No. Put your hands on the bed by your hips," he ordered. His voice was forceful and commanding, sending a pulse of liquid heat straight through her loins. She almost did it, but then stopped herself.

"You're not in charge anymore," she said.

"Oh, I think I am," he said, kneeling down and bringing her hands together behind her back. His face was close to her breasts, and she couldn't help arching her spine and thrusting them forward. He dropped soft kisses along the pale white globes and then tongued his way around the areolas.

She shuddered and shivered, shifting on the bed to try to relieve the ache between her legs. She parted her thighs, and he maneuvered himself forward between them. She felt completely dominated by him physically. He held her hands behind her, forcing her thighs apart with his body as he buried his head between her breasts.

Though she was clearly not in a position of power, his shuddering breath and the way he held her let her know that he was enthralled with her. Her body, which had never seemed to her to be the ideal of beauty, made her proud now. That she could literally bring this strong, domineering man to his knees made her sit a little taller.

She leaned forward and rested her head on top of his, rubbing her cheek against the thickness of his hair as he suckled one of her nipples. She stretched her legs farther apart and then canted her hips forward until she rubbed her center over his erection.

He lifted his head and shifted his body back from hers. Still holding her wrists with one hand, he pushed her skirt to her waist, and she felt him pause as he realized she wore thigh-high hose. He groaned. And then stood up, drawing her to her feet with him.

"Indulge me?" he asked.

"How?" she asked.

"Take off everything," he said.

"What are you going to take off?"

"Nothing."

"That hardly seems fair."

"Sex isn't about fair, it's about what turns us on. And I have a feeling that having me fully dressed while you're bare naked will be a big turn-on for you," he said.

He was right, but that didn't mean she would admit it. It scared her a little how well he seemed to know what she wanted sexually. "I'll do it, but only if you take your shirt off."

"Done," he said, quickly pulling the tank top over his head and then moving to sit in the armchair next to the bed.

He had a lean chest, his well-defined pecs covered with a light dusting of hair. She liked the way he looked, and stood there for a minute drinking him in.

Slowly, keeping her gaze on his, she reached for the zipper at the back of her skirt and tugged it down.

"Is this what you wanted?" she asked.

The skirt slipped lower on her hips, but she kept her stance wide enough that it didn't fall all the way off. Then, when she'd made him wait long enough, she shook her hips and slowly let the skirt fall to the floor.

"Pick up your skirt," he said, not answering her question.

She turned away from him and slowly bent down, watching him over her shoulder as she did so. His eyes narrowed as she reached for the garment and slowly picked it up before tossing it on the bed next to her bra and her shirt.

She shivered a little at the look in his eyes. She slowly pushed her panties down her legs and once again bent to remove them over her boots. He was suddenly there behind her, his hands on her waist and his body bent over hers. She felt the heat of his erection against her buttocks as he pulled her back into the cradle of his hips.

She put her hand out for balance as he rubbed himself against her. He was long and thick and hot. She felt branded by him, and empty as she waited for him to enter her. She was wet and had never been more willing for sex. Ready for him to take her. *And like this,* she thought. She didn't want to have to guard her reactions. She just wanted to let go and enjoy this without worrying if she seemed too vulnerable.

He leaned over her and whispered dark, sexy words into her ear, things that made her even wetter. He told her what he was going to do to her and how deep he was going to take her. She canted her hips back and rubbed herself against him. He took her hands in his and guided them to the footboard, and with their hands joined, she felt him shifting behind her and the tip of him poised to enter him.

"Dammit, give me a second," he said.

He turned away, and she stayed exactly where she was as she heard him open his shaving kit on the nightstand. She glanced over at him to see him opening a condom and putting it on. Later, it would bother her that he had planned for sex, but right now she was grateful.

He was back behind her again, his palms on her waist and his mouth on the back of her neck. He nibbled his way down her spine as he held her still. His hands shifted up to cup her breasts, his fingers pinching lightly at her nipples as he positioned himself behind her again. She felt him shifting between her legs, and one hand lowered to her feminine mound. His finger circled her clit, rubbing lightly. She shifted her hips and moved to where she needed his touch. Then he pulled his hand away, after tapping her lightly with one finger, which made her moan out loud.

She felt him at her entrance again. He teased her with the tip of his erection, and she enjoyed the sensation of his body pressed to hers for a little while, but then the wanting was too much. She arched her back and tried to take him into her body. But he shifted away from her, and she moaned again.

Then he leaned over her, whispering into her ear, "Do you want me?"

"Yes," she said, hating the breathy quality of her own voice. "Dammit, Allan, I need you now. Enough of the games."

"But waiting is the best part," he said, rubbing himself over her again.

"Taking is the best part," she countered.

She heard him groan, and then he plunged into her body in one long, hard stroke that sent the first shivers of orgasm through her. But then he stopped and when she tried to take in more of him, or force him to move, he didn't. He just stayed buried in her body as he kissed her neck and caressed her skin.

But it was too much. She needed him slamming into her and driving her over the edge. She didn't like the feathery sensations that were making the hairs on the back of her neck stand up and shivers course through her.

"Enough waiting," she said. "Take me."

"Not yet." It sounded as if he spoke through gritted teeth.

She tightened herself around him and heard him groan yet again, and then he started moving. His hips rocked with so much force that each thrust drove her forward. She held on tighter to the footboard as he continued moving in and out of her body. Oh, he felt good, she thought as he reached the right spot inside her.

She arched her back to take more of him and keep him hitting her in that delicious spot, as she was so desperate to get to her climax. His breath was hot against her neck and his body warm and sweaty as he moved faster and faster, until she felt the first pulse of her own orgasm. Then he called her name and thrust into her hard for three long strokes, before leaning forward and resting his head between her shoulder blades.

He dropped a kiss on her skin, one so gentle and

tender it made her heart clench. He was supposed to be the arrogant playboy. He wasn't supposed to kiss her like that. He wasn't supposed to be gentle with her. He was supposed to be…well, the Allan she'd always thought him to be.

She shook her head and tried to pretend this orgasm was like any other she'd had, but she knew it was different. She wanted to be a guy about it. To just make some sort of remark about scratching an itch, though inside she knew that this had changed everything between them.

She hated that very fact. Why was it that Allan McKinney, the man she'd always thought of as the devil incarnate, had just made her come harder than anyone else? Or actually made sex seem fun and—

He pulled out of her body, interrupting her thoughts. Unsure what to say, she stood up and looked over at him. They'd just been closer than she'd ever thought they would be, but they were still enemies, she figured. Nothing had changed, yet at the same time everything had.

Allan cursed under his breath and then drew her into his arms, pushing her head down on his shoulder as he hugged her close.

"What are you doing?" she asked.

"Hiding," he said.

"What are you hiding from?"

"You," he said. "You have a way of looking at me that makes me feel like I don't measure up."

His words were a tonic for her weary soul and she struggled to let herself take them at face value. She refused to believe that he'd glimpsed her vulnerability, but at the same time she knew he had, and that there was no way she was going to be able to keep fighting with him and pretending that she loathed him.

The truth was finally forced into the light, she thought. Allan McKinney wasn't her bitter enemy, he was a man. A man she found sexy as hell—and that unnerved her more than she wanted to admit.

Eight

Jessi was jerked awake by the sound of a baby crying. She lay in bed in Allan's arms, not recognizing the strange room for a split second, before she jumped to her feet, grabbed the closest piece of clothing she could find—Allan's shirt—and pulled it on as she ran through the door down the hall to the nursery. Allan was hot on her heels, pulling on his shorts.

They both continued into the nursery, where in the glow of the soft night-light they found Hannah on her back, crying. All her limbs where flailing as she sobbed for all she was worth. They both reached for the baby, but Allan let Jessi pick her up.

She cradled little Hannah against her chest and looked helplessly up at him. "What do you think she needs?"

"I think she might need a bottle. I'll go and warm up the formula while you change her diaper," Allan said.

He left before she could respond. She carried the baby to the table and changed her wet diaper. It bothered Jessi a little that Allan was right. He was probably spot-on about the bottle, too. How was it that he knew more about kids than she did?

She knew he hadn't visited their friends since Hannah was born. They'd both flown out to be there for the birth—and they'd kind of called a truce that day, as well. She remembered how they'd looked at each other in the hospital waiting room when they'd gotten the news about Hannah. They'd almost hugged, but then John was standing there and it had just seemed so awkward.

But for a few moments when they'd been focused on John and Patti, they had sort of gotten along. And then there was little Hannah to hold. And their friends to congratulate.

Hannah was still crying now, and Jessi leaned over the baby. She hummed a tune she'd heard playing earlier on the mobile over Hannah's crib, and then slowly sang words she made up.

"Stop crying, little Hannah. Soon Allan will bring your bottle and you'll go to sleep."

"Here it is," Allan said as he rushed back into the room. "I checked the temperature of the formula on my wrist so I know it's safe for her."

"Great thinking," Jessi said. "I didn't consider that it might be too hot."

He shrugged. "I'm thorough like that. Do you want to feed her or do you want me to?"

"You can do it," she told him.

He came over and scooped the baby up, placing the bottle in her mouth. He stood there next to Jessi while the baby drank eagerly. She brought her little hands up and touched Allan's finger as he held it.

Both adults stared down at Hannah, and Jessi for

her part again felt the heavy loss of John and Patti. "I wonder how often they both stood here like this?" she murmured.

"I was thinking the same thing," Allan said. "It's a sin that we're here and they aren't."

She agreed. Not that she wanted to be dead, but it made no sense that John and Patti had been killed when they had so much to live for. Jessi reached down and touched Hannah's cheek as her little eyes drifted closed, even while she kept drinking her bottle.

"She's so sweet," Jessi said softly. "I'm never going to let anything happen to her."

"Me, either," Allan stated.

She glanced over and noted that he was looking at Hannah as intensely as she was. "You really mean that."

"Of course I do. I gave my word to take care of her," he said.

"Sometimes girls need things that men don't understand," Jessi commented.

He glanced back at her, and she realized too late that she'd revealed something she hadn't intended. "Is that why you're so prickly?"

She smiled a little at the way he said it. "I'm not. I simply get that no one is going to fight my battles for me. At least not the ones that matter to me. And I'm going to make sure that little Hannah here knows she's always got me in her corner. No matter what."

"What battle did you have to fight for yourself?" Allan asked.

"All of them," she said. "But then I'm a bit argumentative, as I'm sure you've noticed."

"With your dad?" he pressed.

"And Granddad. They both had certain ideas about

how a Chandler woman should behave and what she should do."

"Go into gaming and ruin all the Montrose men?" Allan suggested.

Jessi thought about it and wondered if that was the motivation behind her grandfather's desire for her to be so proper. But in the end her family just hadn't worried too much about Thomas Montrose or his heirs. "We didn't really talk about your family that much."

Allan's face tightened. "My grandfather was road-kill to yours, and he never looked back to see the consequences, did he?"

Jessi had never thought of the ousting of Thomas Montrose from the gaming company he'd cofounded with her grandfather that way before, but she could see a certain truth to what Allan said. Gregory Chandler had really cared about only one person and that had been himself. Something he'd passed along to her father.

"Grandfather really wasn't very good at relating to people," Jessi said. "I guess you could say the same about me."

"Nah." Allan walked over to the crib to put the sleeping Hannah down. Jessi joined him as he removed the bottle, and they both sort of held their breath to see if she'd stay asleep.

She did.

Allan looked up at Jessi and smiled, and she smiled back. They had averted a middle-of-the-night crisis. When they got out into the hallway, she started to walk back to her room, but Allan stopped her with a hand on her elbow.

"You're nothing like your grandfather," he said.

"How do you know?"

"By all reports he was a driven man who cared about nothing but the bottom line. Who thought that the people who worked for him were nothing but cogs that kept the machine going. But you aren't like that, Jess. You care about the people around you—I've seen you passionately defend them."

"Yes, you have. I'm amazed John could forgive me for what I did. I did have the best of intentions when I hired that P.I. to investigate his past," Jessi said, trying not to feel all bubbly and warm inside that Allan had called her Jess, an intimate nickname that only her true friends ever used. Maybe it meant nothing, though. It probably was just a slip of the tongue.

"John told me that he couldn't do anything other than forgive you, because you'd been the one to keep Patti safe until he could find her and take over the job. And he said if he'd been anything other than honest with Patti, he wouldn't have deserved to marry her."

"He was truly a great man. Patti was lucky to have fallen in love with him." Jessi felt a lump of emotion in her throat and turned away, but Allan noticed and drew her into his arms, hugging her close. And for the first time since she'd known him she felt a moment's peace in his presence as he eased the ache in her heart.

Allan loosely held the bottle in one hand as he hugged Jessi with his other arm. No matter how hard he tried, it was impossible to keep his distance. They kept having little moments like this one where he couldn't help but see her as a woman. Not his enemy. Not the granddaughter of a man who'd ruined his grandfather's life. Just a girl who'd been wounded, as well.

This was dangerous, he thought. Sex was one thing,

but emotions… He couldn't allow himself to start caring for her. That was when he'd lose the steely grip he'd always had on his control. And he couldn't do that.

Not just because of the situation with Kell and work, but also because of Hannah. If he and Jessi had an affair that involved more than sex, it would end. Everything did. Allan knew this to be the one certainty of his life. And then they'd have to see each other at every important event in Hannah's life.

It would be difficult. More difficult than when their best friends had married and he and Jessi couldn't stand each other. He knew this, yet he also loved the smell of her perfume as she was nestled against his chest. With her head pressed over his heart, for this one second it was easy to forget she was Jessi. Yet at the same time he knew exactly who she was. It was that juxtaposition that made the moment that much more untenable for him. Made it that much harder to drop his arm and move away—something he knew he should do.

Yet he didn't do it. Instead, he let the bottle drop to the floor, so he could wrap both arms around her as she tipped her head back and looked up at him. He saw the same questions in her eyes that were echoing inside him. This was a mistake; they both knew it, yet couldn't stop.

He closed his eyes, trying to remember all the reasons why he needed to let her go, and then he felt the one thing that made it impossible: her lips brushing lightly against his.

"Thanks for being almost human," she said, so softly he had to strain to hear her.

"You're welcome," he said with a chuckle as he opened his eyes and looked at her.

Her gray eyes were cloudy, and for a minute he almost wished he was a different kind of man. One who would know how to soothe the savageness he saw there.

Despite that knowledge of his shortcomings, he hugged her close. "I'm always that way."

She shook her head and put her hand on his shoulder, just a soft light touch as she stayed on her tiptoes, staring into his eyes. He knew she was searching for something—probably answers to the questions that lingered in her own mind—but he had no idea if she'd find them. He wasn't even sure he knew what the answers were.

She opened her mouth, and he put his fingers over her lips. "Don't. We're not going to change this."

She nodded and took his hand in hers and turned to lead him down the hallway in the direction of the room she was using. He followed her even though he knew it wasn't smart. This wasn't a controlled sexual encounter. She was emotional, and he'd be lying if he said he wasn't, too. He already knew there was something else going on inside him. Maybe it was just losing his best friend. Maybe it was—

Who cared? He wasn't going to deny himself Jessi, and he'd figure out everything else later.

She paused on the threshold of her room, turning back to look over her shoulder at him. He realized how irresistible she was with her spiky pixie haircut and that oversize T-shirt that fell to the tops of her thighs.

"Dammit, woman, you're sexy as hell," he said, tracing the hem of the shirt.

"I'm not wearing silk or lace," she said.

"That's probably part of the reason why I find you so hot," he admitted. "It's my shirt."

"This doesn't change anything," she said a warning in her voice.

It changed everything, and she knew it. But by denying it, she was sending him a message that tomorrow they'd be back to acting like the only reason why they were together was because of the their friends' deaths. But last night had changed all that. And there was no going back, no matter what she said now.

He just nodded and picked her up, carrying her into the bedroom and dropping her in the center of the bed. She bounced lightly and arched one eyebrow at him.

"That's not very smooth," she said.

"I'm not smooth or romantic. You know that," he said. He needed to make sure she understood who he was. At heart, he wasn't polished or sophisticated. It didn't matter that he had money and could buy whatever and whoever he wanted. He needed Jessi to understand that growing up in the shadow of hatred had forged him into the kind of man who wasn't gentlemanly. He was a man who'd fought for everything he had, and he doubted if there was a force on earth that could change him.

Not even Jessi Chandler, with her spicy-hot kisses, smooth, pale thighs or strong arms that pulled him closer to her. He knew that she was running from something and using him, but that suited him just fine, because it made it easier to lie to himself and pretend he was using her, too.

Jessi had given in a long time ago to the fact that she often did things that others might deem stupid, such as what she was about to do tonight. But this behavior made her feel alive and distracted her from things that really scared her.

Like how tender Allan had looked holding little Hannah.

Jessi wanted that image out of her head. She wanted him to be a quick lay, and as he stood next to the bed, shoving his shorts down his legs, the last thing she was thinking of was sappy emotional stuff.

She hadn't gotten a chance to really see him when they'd had sex earlier, and as he started to move over her, with one knee on the bed, she reached out to touch his thigh.

She traced the hard muscles with her fingertip, trying to concentrate on that instead of his sex, which jutted toward her. But when she turned her head to look at it, she drew in her breath at the size of him. A shiver of sexual desire coursed through her, making every nerve ending come to attention.

She lifted her hand and wrapped it around the length of his shaft, stroking him up and down until he moved forward to straddle her waist. Then she let go of his sex and raised her hands to his chest.

He was warm, and the light dusting of hair there tickled her fingers as she caressed him. His hands were busy finding the hem of her shirt and tugging it up over her head. He tossed it aside and then looked down at her. He didn't say anything, but leaned forward and slowly swept his hands over her torso to her waist and then lower to her hips, where he squeezed her and held on to her as he rolled to his side and kept her there, pressed against him.

They were both completely naked, and she didn't want to admit it, but they felt right pressed together.

Their bodies just naturally fit, as if they were meant
for each other.

He thrust one thigh between her legs and used his
hands on her hips to draw her forward. As the ridge of
his shaft rubbed all along her feminine core, she shuddered.

She tipped her head back, and he lowered his mouth
to hers as she did so. His kisses were long and languid
and left no room for thoughts of anything but where
his next touch would fall on her body and how long she
could wait before she reached between them and forced
him to enter her.

She swept her hand down his back. It was wide and
smooth, and when she reached lower to cup his buttocks and draw him forward, he groaned her name. She
flexed her fingers, letting him feel the bite of her nails
as she rocked her hips against him.

He shuddered in her arms, and she felt a wave of feminine power washing over her. She exploited it, claimed
it as her own by pushing him onto his back and climbing onto his lap, lifting her mouth from his.

He smiled up at her in an expression she'd never seen
on his face before. Then his hands were on her breasts
as she shifted until the tip of his erection was at the
entrance of her body. It was the feel of his naked flesh
that jarred her and made her realize she was about to
have unprotected sex with him.

She cursed and drew back.

"What's wrong? Oh, the condom."

"I don't have any," she said.

"I do. But I don't want to leave your bed," he said.

She understood that, and she'd always lived with no
regrets. But the impact of the past few hours and real-

izing that she wasn't ready to have a child with this man made her extra cautious. "Well, you're going to have to."

He sighed and rolled out from underneath her. He returned in a quick second with the condom already in place. He climbed into bed and drew her back over his lap. He didn't say anything, just tangled his hands in her short hair and drew her mouth down to his for a passionate kiss that left no doubt that he was still very much turned on.

She put her hands on his shoulders and watched him carefully as she lowered herself onto his shaft and took him completely. His eyes were closed and his neck arched back, and she leaned forward, drawing his head to hers and thrusting her tongue into his mouth as she rode him.

His hands caressed her back, cupping her butt and urging her to quicken her pace, and she did, driving them both toward climax, which she reached instantly. She felt him keep thrusting inside her, and he tore his mouth from hers and leaned down to catch her nipple in his mouth, sucking strongly on it until his hips jerked upward. He gripped her hips, drawing her down hard as he groaned her name.

He turned his face to the side, and she collapsed against him as he held her to his chest, rubbing his palms up and down her back.

She wanted to pretend that nothing had changed, just as she'd said earlier. But as she lay there in his arms and felt the fingers of sleep drawing her in, she realized that everything had changed. She was no longer sure that running away from her emotions was a viable option, because somehow when she hadn't been expecting it, Allan had slipped past her guard.

Nine

Allan woke up with the sun streaming in the windows of an empty bedroom. He knew where he was and remembered clearly holding Jessi in his arms through the night. But she was nowhere to be found this morning.

Neither was Hannah, he discovered after he put on his basketball shorts and checked the nursery. A quick trip to the kitchen revealed Fawkes sipping coffee and doing the *USA TODAY* crossword puzzle on his iPad.

"Good morning, sir. Would you like breakfast?" the butler asked. "Ms. Jessi left a note for you. It's on the counter."

"Coffee's fine," Allan said, waving to Fawkes to keep his seat while he poured his own coffee, which he drank black. "I need to go to John's office this morning and also speak to the funeral home to make sure we're all set for Saturday."

"I have the car ready to go. Ms. Jessi asked me to pick her up at Hatteras Island Care Home at noon. Will that accommodate your plans?" Fawkes asked.

Allan nodded. Well, that explained where Jessi was.

She must have taken Hannah to see her grandmother. "I'm going to shower and then we can leave."

"Yes, sir."

Allan took the note and his coffee mug back to the bedroom he was using. He settled onto the edge of his bed and unfolded the piece of paper.

> Allan,
> I took Hannah to visit Amelia at the Hatteras Group Care Home. I'm not sure she'll recognize us, but I wanted to go and chat with her to see if I could make her understand Patti is gone. I hope you don't mind, but I asked Fawkes to drive us there and pick us up. The man was just sitting around waiting for you to wake up.

The letter was signed with a big *J*.

Just as he'd expected, there was nothing about last night. Underneath their obvious differences, they were very similar, he thought as he gathered his clothes and showered and shaved. They both ignored anything that might make them seem weak. And emotions were definitely something that could do that.

He checked his email and saw that Jessi had been busy sending in a revised promotion plan. He'd been cc'd on one of the exchanges between her and Kell that mentioned three meetings she'd set up via Skype to talk to a production company in Hollywood who were producing a new movie franchise based on a string of very popular books. She'd also managed to arrange a meeting with Jack White, one of the hottest producer-directors in town.

He admired her initiative and wondered when she'd

had time to do all that work. While he'd been sleeping? It bothered him that she might have seen him so relaxed in her arms. Because he knew that it had been a long time since he'd felt that laid-back and had slept so soundly.

He pushed that thought to the back of his mind and instead read the emails that Kell had sent privately to Dec and him.

If she can pull this off we will have to reevaluate our plan to end her employment. Keep me posted, Allan. I need to know about all developments.

Kell didn't seem happy, but at the end of the day he was a fair man, and if Jessi met the terms they'd laid out for her, then Kell would honor his end of the bargain. Allan emailed his cousins back and then got down to business, really analyzing Jessi's plan. He saw that she'd obviously given it some thought. It was almost as if someone different had come up with the plan compared to her offering of a few days ago.

The other proposal had shown someone who didn't really care, but this new plan had innovation and real drive behind it. He'd be lying if he said he wasn't impressed. What had made her change her mind?

And it was clear to him that something had. But he didn't have time to dwell on it. Instead, he left for John's storage unit in town to start sorting through a lifetime's worth of stuff his friend had kept there. John and Patti had left behind high-powered careers to open the bed-and-breakfast, Patti as a highly sought after interior designer and John as a corporate lawyer.

When Allan got to the facility and started sorting

through boxes from his friend's life and career, he realized that he finally got why John had left it all behind.

If his friend had still been living in L.A. and hadn't married Patti, these boxes would be all that he'd left behind. Things that had been generated by long hours spent working for someone else. A life lived on someone else's terms.

Mostly it was John's private notes on his clients. Stuff that wasn't part of his official work files. Things about their habits and how they liked to have their paperwork prepared.

Allan shook his head, surprised that John's death was making him reevaluate his own life and choices. But there was one key difference between his friend and him, and that was Patti. John had found his soul mate, a woman who shared his vision of the future and what life should look like. Allan hadn't found anyone like that and doubted he ever would.

He liked being just a little bit selfish and answering to no one save himself when he wanted to do something. It was an attitude he doubted he'd ever lose.

He rubbed the back of his neck as he got a text message from Fawkes informing him that he was going to have to leave to go and pick up Jessi and Hannah. Suddenly, Allan didn't want to keep sorting through files. He wanted to see Jessi and ascertain for himself if she had changed.

There was something different about her note and emails from this morning, and he was curious as to what it was. He told himself it was important that he figure it out so he could advise Kell and keep Playtone Games on top, but he knew that wasn't the only reason he wanted to see her.

He missed her. He hated that he'd woken up alone, and he wanted to see if she was running from him. It could be construed as cowardly, but to him it had seemed as if Jessi had beat a strategic retreat to regroup and refocus.

He wondered why she'd done it. One thing was certain—if it was a calculated move, she'd been successful, because all he'd done this morning was think about her.

Jessi had been running on adrenaline and nerves all morning.

The house where Amelia lived looked from the outside like another bed-and-breakfast, but as soon as she stepped inside, the smell of antiseptic let her know it was a nursing home.

"Hello," the duty nurse said in greeting as she came inside.

Jessi carefully shifted Hannah so she could reach out to shake the nurse's hand. "Hi, I'm Jessi Chandler. Patti McCoy was my best friend and I'm here with her daughter, Hannah, to visit Amelia Pearson."

"Have a seat over there and I'll call for Sophie, Mrs. Pearson's care nurse."

Jessi took a seat and five minutes later a woman wearing crepe-soled shoes and a floral dress came over to her. "Hi, I'm Sophie. I understand you're here to see Mrs. Pearson."

"Yes. Would that be okay?"

"Let's go into my office and talk. There are some things you should know. Who is this little cutie?"

"This is Hannah. She's Amelia's granddaughter," Jessi said.

Hannah made a sweet little coo as Sophie tickled

her chin. Then the nurse led the way into her office. "Please have a seat."

Jessi did. "I don't want to create a problem, but I would feel better if I could talk to Amelia myself and make sure she understands about Patti."

"We've already let Mrs. Pearson know about her daughter's death."

"I figured you had, but I wouldn't feel right if I didn't talk to her myself."

"She's having a good day, so I think we can arrange it. The most important thing for you to do is not agitate her. I'm going to give you a pamphlet to read over while I go and see if she'd like to have visitors."

Jessi read the pamphlet and felt a knot tighten in the pit of her stomach. It made her sad to think that the woman who'd always been so kind to her and treated her like a second daughter was lost in a world that was so confusing.

"Okay, we're all set. She remembers you and is looking forward to talking to you," Sophie said.

"Great," Jessi said, following the nurse into the solarium, where Mrs. Pearson was already seated in a fan-backed rattan chair.

"Jessi. How wonderful to see you," Amelia said as soon as she walked in. The older woman stood up to hug her.

"Look at this baby. Is it yours?" Amelia asked.

"No, she's Patti's daughter," Jessi said, careful to keep her tone quiet and calm, as the brochure had recommended.

Sophie stood in the corner observing them, which made the situation all the more surreal.

"May I hold your baby?" Amelia asked.

Sophie nodded, so Jessi got up and handed the baby to her grandmother. What was truly surprising was how she reached for Hannah and then held the baby so tenderly.

Jessi took her iPhone out of her pocket while Amelia was staring down at the baby and talking to herself, and after making sure it was on silent, took a quick picture, knowing that Hannah might want to see this someday.

Jessi carefully sat back down, and Amelia looked over at her. "Patti is the best baby. Her father's gone a lot but she never fusses."

Jessi glanced over at Sophie in confusion, but then remembered how the brochure had said to restate facts but not to argue. "Patti was a great a baby. This is her daughter, Hannah. She's a little bit of a stinker sometimes, but also a great baby."

"Hannah? My best friend growing up was Anna. I haven't talked to her in years," Amelia said.

"That happens as we get older," Jessi said. "You know Patti was my best friend, right?"

"Yes, I do. Patti is so lucky to have found you as her friend. I remember the first time you came to our home, when you two were in elementary school. You'd been in a fight."

Jessi nodded. She'd been a mess back then. She'd been defending Cari from some boys who used to pull on her long blond ringlets. Jessi had torn her shirt and knew she'd get in trouble at home if she came in looking like that, so Patti had brought her to her house instead. "You were very kind to me, Mrs. Pearson. You fixed my blouse and gave me cookies and promised not to tell my dad I'd been in a fight."

"Well, I could see you needed some love."

Jessi swallowed hard. She had just needed to feel accepted for herself instead of always being the middle Chandler girl, part of a unit instead of an individual. And Patti's mom had done just that.

"Patti is sleeping a lot today. She won't sleep tonight," Amelia said.

"It's okay if *Hannah* sleeps a lot, Amelia. I'm sure she'll sleep tonight."

"No, she won't," Amelia said. "Derek will be mad if the baby cries at night. He needs his sleep."

"It's okay. This is Hannah, not Patti," Jessi said again, seeing Sophie move quickly toward them as Amelia started shaking Hannah.

Jessi jumped up and took Hannah from her grandmother as the baby started crying. Sophie rushed over and tried to calm Amelia, who was now agitated by the baby's cries. Jessi tucked little Hannah against her shoulder and rubbed her back, trying to soothe her.

"It's okay, Amelia," the care nurse was saying. "Ms. Chandler, why don't you step outside? One of the staff will take you to see the doctor on duty."

Jessi went into the hall and found a nurse waiting there, along with two technicians, who went into the solarium to help subdue Amelia. Jessi's heart ached as she watched the woman who'd once taken such good care of her falling to pieces.

Hannah was still crying, and Jessi reached into the Vera Bradley diaper bag and found her pacifier, which the baby latched on to as soon as it was in her mouth.

"I think I'd better have a doctor check Hannah out. Amelia shook her," Jessi said to the nurse.

"I'll take you to him. Are you okay?"

"Yes. But I didn't get to tell her that Patti is dead. I don't think she understands that."

"We've informed her, and her care nurse will keep reminding her of those things when it's needed."

Jessi knew there was nothing more she could do. But seeing Mrs. Pearson in such a state made her glad her own mother's struggle with cancer had ended quickly. Jessi would have hated to see her suffering the way Amelia was.

The doctor on duty was a GP.

"I'm Dr. Gold," he said when he entered. "I heard you had a little incident?"

"Yes," Jessi said. "Hannah was shaken and I just want to make sure she's okay."

"I can check her out. Put her on the bed over there, but keep holding her little hands."

He examined Hannah, making comments to the baby as he worked. Then he looked over at Jessi. "She's going to be just fine."

"Thank you, Doctor."

Jessi had already texted Fawkes to come and pick them up, but he wasn't there when she stepped out into the sunny October day. She tipped her face to the sun and held the baby.

When the car pulled up about five minutes later, she almost groaned as she noted that Fawkes wasn't at the wheel. It was Allan. He got out and pushed his sunglasses up on his head.

"You okay?"

"Yes. Amelia had an episode, so we had to end our visit early," Jessi said. She couldn't recount any more of it since she was still shaken by what had happened.

"What kind of episode?" Allan asked, opening the door to the backseat and reaching for Hannah.

Jessi passed the baby to him and noticed that he dropped a quick kiss on her forehead before putting her into the car seat, fastening her in and then tucking her stuffed frog next to her cheek.

"What kind of episode, Jessi?" Allan asked again as he closed the door.

Jessi realized she'd been staring at him. She didn't like that he kept her off-kilter all the time lately. She mentally gave herself a slap, the type Cher gave herself in *Moonstruck,* and told herself to snap out of it.

"She was worried the baby was sleeping too much and shook her awake. Then she got really agitated when I took the baby and Hannah kept crying. I had to leave so the nurse and some technicians could calm her down," Jessi said.

"She shook Hannah?" Allan asked.

"Yes, but the doctor on duty checked her out, and she's fine. I also was informed before I left that Amelia has been sedated and is sleeping now."

Allan held her door open for her, and Jessi seated herself. She watched him walk around to the driver's side and get behind the wheel. He started the engine and then turned to her.

"It had to be difficult to see that happening with Patti's mom."

"It was, but it just underscored that we're all the family Hannah has now. Amelia will never be a grandmother to her," Jessi said.

"We'll be good to Hannah," Allan said. "Together we will make sure she has all the family she needs."

He'd made them a team, a family, and Jessi didn't

know what to say. She was silent as he drove down the little two-lane road back to the bed-and-breakfast. She really didn't know how she felt about being linked to Allan McKinney for the rest of her life. The part that was upsetting was that it didn't bother her as much as she would have thought it should.

While Jessi put Hannah down for a nap, Allan took some iced tea that Fawkes had made to the porch and then quickly read another chapter in one of the baby care books he'd downloaded to his phone.

"Whatcha reading?" Jessi asked as she came and sat next to him on one of the large pine rockers.

"Uh, nothing," he said. "I saw your aggressive plan to win over some business with the producer Jack White."

"I know it's bold, but, hey, that's my style. He was more than happy to take the appointment when I appealed to his sense of fairness."

"How did you do that?"

"I simply reminded him that at one time he was making small, independent films and he'd had to rely on bigger names to help him along. One of them was my grandfather, who invested a lot of money in what he called *Project 17* back then."

"I didn't know your grandfather did that," Allan said. The Montroses had focused a lot of time on studying the ins and outs of Gregory Chandler's business, but only his gaming stuff. Allan supposed his grandfather hadn't been interested in anything but that. However, this was key information they should have had.

"Well, he did. *Project 17* went on to become his first blockbuster, *Cowboys from Space*...so I appealed to his sense of fair play and asked for a meeting."

"And you got it. I like that you didn't hesitate to go after it, but I'm curious about something," Allan said. He glanced over at her. She was wearing a pair of white shorts that hit her midthigh and a sleeveless top that was fitted over her breasts and then fell loosely around her stomach. She'd put on a denim jacket to combat the breeze. Her sandals had a slight heel. For once, she didn't look all rocker chick, but instead looked like any other woman on the island.

He felt as if something was changing in Jessi and he wondered what, exactly, it was and how he could use it to his own advantage. Because no matter what changed, his reflex was to assume that they were still at war and always would be. Or were they? Had last night changed her enough to call a real truce?

He had woken up with the feeling that something was different in himself, but then when he'd found her gone... Dammit, he hated when he got petty, but had just realized he was bothered by the fact that she'd left him alone in her bed.

"What?"

"Well, two things," he said.

She arched her eyebrows and gave him a look that said to get on with it. He realized she hadn't changed as much as he'd previously thought and wondered again if the change was in him and not her. He hoped not.

"What caused your new attitude toward Playtone-Infinity Games? Don't deny something has changed— last week you didn't use your old contact with Jack White. So why now?" he asked.

"Hannah," she said. "I'm going to be her mother fig-ure now, and I know that kids get a lot more from what we do than from what we say we do. So if I told her to always do her best, no matter what the situation, but she knew that I'd sort of phoned it in at the end and let myself be fired…well, I just don't want her thinking that."

"How would she ever know about this? She's only three months old," Allan said, pushing his sunglasses up on his forehead and turning to face Jessi.

"I figured you'd mention it. I just didn't want it to be an issue. What was your second question?" she asked, leaning back in the chair and looking out toward the Pamlico Sound.

"I'm not ready to let you change the conversation," he said.

"Too bad," she replied. "Do you have another question or not?"

"Actually, I do. Why didn't you wake me up this morning?"

She sat up slowly, nibbling her bottom lip for a second before she seemed to realize what she was doing. She straightened her shoulders and looked at him. "You don't seem like the type of guy who wants a clingy woman, and goodness knows I don't cling."

"Liar," he said. He could hear the bravado and the challenge in her voice.

"Why did you come to my bed last night?" she asked. "And don't say it was just physical."

Allan knew there were two ways he could play this. One was blustery and posturing, and the other was… honest.

He reached out and took her hand in his. "Because I couldn't help myself. I don't know what it is about you, Jessi Chandler, but you always cause me to act in a way… Let's just say you make me forget myself."

"I do? I don't believe that," she said. "I think you get

a wild feeling and just can't resist following it to see what happens."

"I'm not that unpredictable," he said. "Most of the time when it comes to you I just won't back down, because I know you'd see it as a sign of weakness. And like you said earlier, actions speak way louder than words."

"I never see you as weak," she admitted, her voice a little bit softer, all that challenge and bravado ebbing away.

But it wasn't entirely gone, and he realized then something about Jessi that had been abundantly clear from the first moment he'd met her, even though he'd never taken notice of it before. She was always on the edge and ready to jump off. And now he had to decide if he was going to let go and watch or join her for the crazy ride.

Ten

They fell into a sort of rhythm over the days after the funeral. Kell hadn't come but Dec, Cari and Emma all had. It was very somber, and she had been glad to have her sisters there, but their stay had been too brief—they flew in and out on the same day.

She'd hoped that Reggie would have the custody all wrapped up so they could go back to L.A. by now, but the judge didn't move quickly. And then there was the storm in the Atlantic to contend with. First the predictions had the storm going toward Florida, and then into the Gulf of Mexico, but it had stalled out and now a stronger storm was taking its place, this one aiming straight for the Atlantic Seaboard.

Focusing on hurricane preparedness gave Jessi an excuse not to dwell on Allan. Which was difficult, because the last thing she wanted was for any of this to start to feel normal. But that was exactly what had happened. Worst of all, she couldn't wait to wake up each morning and have coffee with Allan while Fawkes did his crossword and baby Hannah drank her bottle.

He was quiet in the morning until he'd had his first

cup of coffee, which had surprised her because he was so chatty the rest of the time. And Fawkes had thawed toward her. If she had to pinpoint the moment when it had happened, she thought it was at the funeral, when she'd wrapped her arm around Allan's shoulders to keep him from breaking down. She didn't like to remember that moment when he'd seemed all too human and vulnerable.

But that time had passed and she was well aware that they were existing in a sort of vacuum as they waited for the custody of Hannah to be approved, and they wrapped up the rest of Patti and John's business matters. Fall seemed just around the corner. Jessi had even surprised herself by buying a tiny Halloween costume for Hannah to wear—an Elvis wig and leather jacket, which she thought would crack Allan up.

They had become that family unit she'd sort of been afraid of, and yet at the same time they hadn't. There was a tension between the two of them that couldn't be explained away. And no matter how nice it was to sit quietly in the kitchen in the morning, usually the rest of the day would reinforce in one way or another that they were still members of two different families embroiled in a feud.

It looked as if Jessi wouldn't be able to get back to L.A. for the meeting with Jack White, and Kell wasn't budging on his timeline. For an entire day she'd debated returning and giving up her rights to Hannah, but in the end she realized she'd only decided to try to keep her job at the merged company for Hannah's sake, so it made no sense to sacrifice her.

On Tuesday morning, Allan and Jessi were sitting at the kitchen table with Hannah and Fawkes, settling into their usual routine, when Allan asked, "Why are you staring at me?"

"I'm still marveling at the fact that you can be quiet for more than a second," Jessi said. "Every morning it's like discovering a new treasure."

He lowered his eyebrows, but didn't say anything, just took another sip of his coffee and went back to reading the *Wall Street Journal* on his iPad. Or at least that's what she thought he was reading, until Hannah slammed down her bottle and formula splattered across the table and onto the tablet. Jessi grabbed a towel and leaned over to wipe it off, noticing in the process that he was reading a book.

"You rat," she said.

"What?"

"*Baby 411!* That's what you've been reading every morning? No wonder you're so much better with Hannah than I am."

"I'll take Miss Hannah into the other room," Fawkes said as he got her out of her baby seat.

"Why?" Allan asked.

"She shouldn't hear you two fighting," he said as he walked away.

"Are we going to be fighting?" Allan asked when they were alone.

"I don't want to, but honestly, why would you go behind my back like that?" Jessi said. "I wondered why you knew what to do, but I figured you were going on gut instinct like me. Is being able to best me so important to you?"

"I don't like to lose," he said with a shrug, putting the cover over his iPad before standing up and taking his mug over to the Keurig machine. He made himself another cup of coffee as she watched him.

"I thought things were changing between us, but you're still the same," she said as he leaned back against the kitchen counter.

He stared down into his cup before putting it down. "I'm not the same. I downloaded the book because I knew nothing and was totally afraid I'd do something wrong. I can't be in a situation without knowing as much as I can about it."

"Why not just say that? Or suggest I read up on baby care? Clearly, I'm not a natural mother," Jessi said.

"Jess, you are wonderful with Hannah. Even when you screw up, you course correct and make it into something that is okay."

"Still, I wish you'd said something."

"If I had suggested you read a book on baby care you would have exploded and told me not to boss you around," he said.

"True. But I thought you were just supersmart when it came to kids," she said. "I'm kind of glad you're not. I was beginning to think you really were the superman you believe yourself to be."

"Ah, now you see the chinks in my armor? I suspect you knew they were there from the first moment we met," he said.

She thought back to that day. She'd never in her life been so scared. Her best friend had found her soul mate, and Jessi had known that she and Patti would never be as close again. And then there was sexy Allan acting all chummy with Patti and John. Jessi had heard of him before because of their family history, but hadn't ex-

pected him to be this obnoxious. She'd felt isolated…
left out again, and it hurt.

"Only once you started talking," she said.

He threw his head back and laughed. "You're a pain
in the ass. You know that, right?"

"I try. So what's that book say about when she can
have real food?" Jessi asked, because she'd rather talk
about the baby than about him and her. It had been so
hard to keep her distance for the past week, but she'd
done it because she already liked Allan too much, and
allowing the physical bond between them to get any
stronger would only lead her down the path to love.

And that frightened her more than anything else
she'd experienced in her entire life. She just didn't think
she was ready to give over her heart and her happiness
to a man who kept so much of himself hidden.

"Let me look," he said.

She watched him for a minute and then realized what
she was doing. "I'll go get Fawkes and Hannah."

She left the room without looking back.

Allan didn't dwell on feelings; he'd never been that
comfortable with emotion. And nothing that he'd experienced since he'd arrived on Hatteras had changed
his mind. Emotions were uncomfortable and created a
lot of stress. The more he cared for Hannah and Jessi,
the more he worried about them. Over the past few
days he'd tried a couple times to lure Jessi back to bed,
but she'd resisted, and frankly, he thought that was for
the best.

What he needed was to get back to L.A. so he could
have a little distance from Jessi. In terms of finalizing
custody of Hannah, he was rattling cages, but he had

no connections in North Carolina, and the local judge wasn't going to be rushed. Even though Patti and John had asked in their will that Jessi and he become guardians, the state wouldn't simply give the baby over to them without paperwork and visits. They'd had two in-home visits, and Reggie was doing all he could to speed the process along, but Allan was ready to get back to California.

He wanted life to return to normal. He'd never admit it aloud, but he was starting to like the routine of living with Jessi. Hannah was the sweetest thing, too, and he felt safe admitting that he loved that little baby as if she was his own daughter. But there was something almost surreal about sharing that bond with Jessi.

She'd changed since they'd been here. Her rocker chick clothes had given way to a wardrobe of casual jeans and blousy shirts. He realized she'd brought them with her, so she must have just been wearing her badass clothes to rile him.

Which she had. And that was part of the problem between the two of them. She was fire where he was concerned, and though he knew he'd get burned, he kept moving closer to her. In fact, he didn't mind being singed by her heat.

"Allan, you better come in here," Jessi called from the living room.

He went into the other room and saw that she was sitting on the floor playing with Hannah, while Fawkes sat in one of the armchairs. But they were both watching the television.

"What's up?"

"Hurricane warning. One of the tracking models has it heading straight for us."

"Great. I'm going to call Reggie and see if this will finally convince the judge to move on the custody ruling," Allan said.

"Let's switch over to the Weather Channel and see what it means for us. I think that the models are often unpredictable," Jessi said.

"Even if the Weather Channel has a different prediction, we don't want to take any chances," Allan said. "We both want to get back home, right, Jessi?"

She nodded, but there was something in her expression that made him wonder for a moment if she might not be in that big a hurry. But he doubted it. She had her own life, and the other night she herself had said that it would be easier with Hannah once they got back into their own routines.

He left her with Fawkes and walked back to his room to make the call. Allan sat on the edge of his bed and pondered whether he should try to convince Jessi to sell the bed-and-breakfast. He didn't think they were going to be able to manage it from across the country.

"Reggie Blythe." The attorney answered his phone on the second ring.

"Reggie, this is Allan McKinney. We just saw the weather bulletin about the possible hurricane. Any chance this will help the judge hurry his decision?"

"I was thinking along the same lines and already sent my secretary over to see if we can get on the docket for today or tomorrow. You and Jessi will need to leave the island if there is an evacuation."

"Really?"

"Yes, it's illegal for a nonresident to stay on Hatteras if that happens," Reggie said. "I think maybe the weather is going to work in your favor."

"I hope so. We want the right decision for Hannah, but we're also ready to get back home. Hannah needs to start adjusting to her new environment."

"I agree. I'll let you know as soon as we hear something more," Reggie said.

"One more thing," Allan said. "What does John and Patti's will say about the bed-and-breakfast? Does it have to be held for Hannah until she comes of age? Can Jessi and I sell it and put the money aside for her?"

"I'll look into it, but I do know that John hoped you'd keep the place open," Reggie said.

"That's all well and good, but neither Jessi nor I know a thing about running a hotel. I'm just trying to figure out what makes sense," Allan said. "I want to honor John's wishes…."

"I'll see what I can come up with. I might be able to find a caretaker for the property who can be paid out of the profits until Hannah is of age," Reggie suggested.

"That might work. Let me know if I can help in any way."

"I will."

He ended the call and then dialed Kell's number.

"What's up, Allan?"

"It looks like the hurricane in the Atlantic is headed straight for us," he said.

His cousin gave a mirthless laugh. "Seems like Jessi is never going to get back to L.A."

"It actually might speed up our leaving the island. We are using it as a reason to force the judge to make a decision. I just wanted to keep you posted."

"Thanks," Kell said.

"Kell?"

"Yeah?"

"Why do you hate Jessi so much?" Allan asked. It was one thing to have been upset about what happened with the past generation, and he knew that Jessi could be irritating, but he had no idea why his cousin didn't like her.

"Because she's a Chandler. I don't know her personally," Kell said.

"She's a great woman, Kell. Talented and dedicated to the company—"

"Don't tell me you've fallen for her. You hate her. You said she's a pain in the ass," Kell said.

"I did, didn't I." But he finally realized that "hating" Jessi had been a self-defense maneuver to protect himself, because she was too easy to respect and like and fall for.

"Yes. So don't desert me," his cousin declared. "I have to listen to Dec telling me how great all the Chandlers are every time we get together."

"I won't. I'm still staunchly a Montrose heir."

"Good to hear it," Kell said and ended the call.

Fawkes went out for supplies, and Jessi called a local handyman to see if he could come and make the bed-and-breakfast hurricane-ready. He was listed in the notebook where Patti had kept all the local services she used, including housekeeping and lawn maintenance.

"I'll be there as soon as we know it's headed this way," James the handyman said. "I know that property well, since it was in my family before the McCoys purchased it."

"Have you considered acting as a caretaker here?" Jessi asked, remembering that Allan had floated that as a possibility.

"Perhaps. I have my own business now and I'd have to ask the wife," he said. "She gets mighty pissed if I don't run things past her first."

Jessi smiled to herself. "How long have you been married?"

"Twenty years. Still feels like we just got back from our honeymoon," he said.

She smiled to herself. Happy couples made her feel better about the possibilities. And then she realized that for the first time she wasn't thinking of love and to-getherness in vague terms, but specifically in terms of herself and Hannah and Allan.

His faults still loomed in the back of her mind, and she knew he hadn't said a word about them dat-ing when they returned to California, but a part of her knew things had changed between them.

She thought back to this morning in the kitchen, when he'd admitted, well, that he was human. That he had flaws and that he didn't want her to see them. It was enough to fan the flames of the secret desire in her heart. She wasn't entirely sure when something as ill-advised as falling for Allan had started to be…well, something she wanted.

She liked that her heart raced every time he entered a room or that she got a little thrill from flirting with him and teasing him. True, she'd been cautious and tried to keep him at arm's length, but a part of her was very sure that Allan and she were…what?

Even to herself she couldn't admit it. Even in her own head she was afraid to let it be true.

She was falling in love with Allan.

Hannah made her little gurgling noises, and Jessi smiled over at the tiny baby. She scooped her up and held her in her arms, leaning close to take a deep breath of the fresh clean baby smell.

"You did good, Patti," she said out loud. She hadn't let herself hold Hannah or even talk to Patti about the baby much when her friend had been alive. Jessi had always thought she'd lived her life on her terms—no fears, no regrets—but now she realized how paralyzing that lie and the fear underlying it had been. It had been strong enough to make her miss out on sharing this joy with Patti because she'd been terrified of even holding the newborn.

Her entire self-view shifted in that instant, and Jessi understood that she'd been cowardly her entire life. Being here with Hannah was making it crystal clear how much she'd missed by keeping everyone at bay. Instead of facing the things that scared her, she'd fought with them, told herself she didn't need them and walked away.

She'd done it this morning in the kitchen. When her gut had told her to move toward Allan she'd backed away.

Hannah was starting to get sleepy, her little eyes drifting closed, and for a moment Jessi debated sitting on the porch and just holding the little girl. But then she decided she wanted to get some work done.

She took Hannah upstairs, stopping under the picture of Patti and John that Allan had hung above the crib. It had just appeared there two days ago. And when she'd asked him about it, he said that he didn't want her to forget their faces.

It had been a sweet sentiment, but then he'd spoiled the moment by making a pass at her. Now that she thought back on it, Jessi realized that Allan ran from emotion the same way she did.

Maybe that meant that he was starting to care for her. She put Hannah in her crib and sat down in the rocking chair to think. Was she going to keep running away from life or was she going to be the woman she'd always believed herself to be and face the thing that scared her the most?

Ironically, it was Allan. She'd fought with him and dared him and taunted him since the moment they'd met, and it was only now that she could recognize she'd done all of those things to keep herself from falling for him. And they hadn't exactly been successful. There had always been a part of her that had wanted to see him again.

She pushed herself up from the chair, resolute in her conviction that she wasn't going to run anymore.

Walking down the hallway to his bedroom, she paused on the threshold as she realized he was on the phone. She didn't want to eavesdrop, but heard him say that he was still a true Montrose heir.

Jessi knew better than to listen at doors, but she couldn't deny what she'd overheard. It was a fierce reminder of something that she already knew. No matter how he acted when he was here, he was still her… frenemy.

Eleven

She started for the stairs, but then remembered her new promise to herself. No more running away.

Resolutely, she strode back to Allan's room and found him still sitting on the edge of the bed, looking contemplative.

"So you're a staunch Montrose heir?" she asked.

"That's not exactly news," he said, tossing his phone on the bed and standing up. "Why were you eavesdropping?"

"Sorry. I didn't mean to. I kind of thought we'd changed in our attitudes toward each other…well, at least I know that I have. I no longer view you as one of those nasty Montroses."

She put her hands on her hips and looked at him, daring him to lie to her.

"You're right. We have changed toward each other. But at the end of the day we're still business rivals— no, that's the wrong word. But things aren't going to magically fix themselves. I know you're working hard to change Kell's image of you, but it's still down to financial gain as far as he's concerned," Allan said.

What exactly was he saying? "You're not being very clear. Even if I get Jack White to agree to a deal, the money won't come in this quarter or probably even the next. Is all that work for nothing? Because I'm fine with not keeping that meeting and letting you guys go hang," she said.

"That's not what I was saying. Potential profit will satisfy the terms of your probation," Allan said. "Why are you being so argumentative?"

"You shook me. I've just been thinking about my life and myself, and I made some discoveries I didn't necessarily find comfortable. But I was thinking you and me—we'd both… Never mind. I just sound like some sappy schoolgirl."

"You are the furthest thing from sappy I've ever met. Finish your thought," he said, closing the gap between them and touching her chin. "I like you when you are at your most honest."

"I like that quality in you as well, but I don't get to see that guy as often as I'd like."

He dropped his hand and thrust it through his thick hair. "What do you want me to say? I learned early on that when you care for someone they have power over you."

"Do I have power over you?" She felt a shot of pure adrenaline as she asked the question that had been burning in the back of her mind since that kiss they'd shared on his plane. Living so openly and so honestly gave her a rush of excitement, but she also saw the potential for a lot of pain.

"You know you do," he said. "All week I've been trying to get you back into my bed, but you keep pushing me away. Why is that? Do I have some sort of power over *you?*"

He wanted to keep things even and she couldn't blame him, but with her new knowledge she realized that if she was truly living bold and large she couldn't hedge her bets or hesitate. She had to go all-in.

"Yes, you do," she said quietly. "And it's not just about sex, but influences every corner of my life. I really hope that I'm not just making you into the man I want you to be, because you are becoming very important to me."

Allan looked at her in shock. She saw the fear in his eyes—or at least that's what she hoped it was, because otherwise it might be pity.

Oh, please don't let it be pity.

He stepped back from her, turned away and walked over to the window that overlooked the garden in the backyard.

"I don't know what to say to that," he said after a few minutes had passed.

"It's not that hard," she said softly. "If you're honest with yourself you know exactly what to say, and if you're brave enough you'll be able to say it."

She heard the dare in her words and decided she was okay with that. She couldn't completely change her attitude in one day. And if he was man enough to be with her, man enough to actually be there for her as she really hoped he would, then he'd have to be as honest with her as she'd been with him.

"I… You want something from me that I've given no one else, not even my parents or my best friend," Allan said, still not facing her.

She saw the proud set of his shoulders and thought

that he'd never be able to say the words she desperately wanted to hear. She hesitated and wondered if him saying them made a difference to what she was already feeling, and knew that it didn't.

Her heart sped up as she walked over and put her arms around him, linking them together over his chest as she rested her head between his shoulder blades. He was tense for a few seconds, but then brought his hand up to cover hers. He didn't say another word, and neither did she.

For this moment it was enough. She didn't need to hear the words from him, but the small knot in the pit of her stomach warned that she would need to sooner or later, and she only hoped that he'd be able to give them to her when it was time.

He turned in her embrace and stepped away from her, and that tiny knot grew as she realized that her gamble hadn't paid off. Allan wasn't the man she thought he was. She'd taken a chance on love and in the end it would have been better if she'd simply kept running from the emotion, because it seemed it wasn't for her.

"We've got a lot to do," he said at last.

"Of course," she replied, swallowing hard. "I've called a handyman to come and make the house hurricane-ready. He's waiting until the final warnings are issued. Also, he might be interested in applying to be the caretaker here."

Allan nodded.

Jessi turned and walked out the door, hoping he'd call her back and pretending she wasn't disappointed when he didn't.

Allan almost wished he was a different type of man. The kind of guy who'd run after Jessi and bring her

back. But he wasn't. And he knew he couldn't be. He'd
seen his father devote himself solely to one person's
happiness, and in the end that devotion had killed him.
His dad hadn't been able to live without his mom.

He knew that women often thought that was romantic or sweet, but he'd seen the other side of it. How his
father wouldn't leave the house for days while his mom
was on business trips. His dad had a career of his own,
but had been crippled by loneliness when his mother
had traveled out of town. And then there was the almost
manic way he'd act when she was back. He'd never let
her leave his sight. That kind of dependence on someone was something Allan vowed to never experience.

He had promised himself a long time ago that he'd
never let any woman have that control over him. And
if he was being completely honest with himself he'd
have to admit that Jessi was already starting to make
him feel a little like that. He refused to let it go further.

If he hurt her feelings now, he was sorry, but he knew
that in the end no woman could live with that kind of
obsessive love. He wasn't guessing or speculating; his
mother had told him that when she'd left their family
home to go back to her own father. It was just an odd
twist of fate that she'd died in a car crash on her way
there.

Allan rubbed the back of his neck. Damn, he never
thought about those two—his parents, who had been
so doomed in love. He had plenty of other things to oc-
cupy his mind. The hurricane brewing out in the Atlantic. Finding a caretaker for this place. Raising baby
Hannah. And what to do about Jessi.

There was no way that he could force her from his
thoughts. And part of him feared that he might be just

like his dad, because the past few days had proved how much he really enjoyed being in her company. Every morning he got out of bed a little more easily than he ever had before, and actually looked forward to sitting in the quiet kitchen with her across the table from him.

There was something about her that called to him, and no matter what he said or how he acted toward her, he couldn't change that. So that made priority number one getting off Hatteras Island and keeping Jessi from satisfying the objectives in her probation. He wanted her to fail—needed her to.

Somehow the thought of seeing her every day at work and in his personal life was too...tempting. And he didn't like it. He'd always known that he wasn't good at personal relationships but he hadn't understood until this moment the real reason.

He didn't like the vulnerability that came with letting someone past his guard. Not just anyone—Jessi. She made him feel weak and unsure because he needed her and that wasn't acceptable.

But he knew he wouldn't be able to force her hand or to *make* her fail. He just had to hope that she ran out of time. It seemed unlikely, given the type of woman she was.

And that made him realize that he also had to decide if he was going to keep his guardianship of Hannah. Maybe he should let that go, as well...though John wouldn't have liked that.

In fact, if his friend were here right now he'd probably punch Allan in the shoulder and tell him to stop acting like an ass.

He paused in front of the mirror and stared at himself. He looked nothing like his father, but that didn't stop him from following in his footsteps where obsession was concerned. His grandfather, too, had been obsessed—with business. Allan didn't want to be like either of the main male influences in his life.

Was it impossible for him not to be like them? It seemed that obsessive personality trait ran deep. He knew from his own rigid attempts at control that he had somehow mastered it after all these years, until Jessi.

She threatened him. Threatened his sanity and his control and his core belief in himself. And now she wanted him to... What exactly did she want? He both admired and envied that she was able to be transparent and come to him and ask how he felt.

He knew that took more courage than he had. Because even though she'd sort of said what she was feeling toward him, he still couldn't bring himself to let her know what she meant to him.

He didn't care if that made him a coward—sure, he'd have kicked anyone's ass who said he was one, but he couldn't deny it to himself. It didn't change anything. He wouldn't let it.

But the words felt hollow and empty as he went downstairs and saw Jessi in the backyard, talking to the handyman and then working beside him to gather up loose articles in the yard.

She wore a pair of ridiculously high heels, skintight jeans and a white tank top paired with a black leather vest. She was back to her rocker chick clothing. He took a deep breath, acknowledging to himself that he was glad.

This was the Jessi he knew how to handle. He could challenge her and bet with her and probably even take her to his bed. She was the woman who gave as good as she got, and never let him forget it.

But another part of him was sad. He realized he'd missed a chance with Jessi. A chance to really know her and maybe find some sort of happiness.

Who was he kidding? He'd never really be happy. Not with Jessi Chandler. Not just because of the Chandler connection, but also because she did challenge him and dare him, and she'd never have settled for only half of what he was. She'd never have accepted the small bit of himself he'd have felt comfortable giving her, and a part of him was glad.

Because the way he felt about her, he wanted her to have it all. All the happiness and love that she deserved. And he knew he wasn't the man to give it to her.

With the hurricane warning slowly turning into a real threat, James had suggested they go ahead and do a few preventive things, such as get anything loose in the yard stored. And since it was either work with her hands or choke Allan, Jessi decided to dig in and help. She had the baby monitor speaker attached to her hip as she worked, putting away hoses and chairs and piling up loose tree limbs.

She could see as she puttered about the yard why her friend had enjoyed this pace after years of working eighteen-hour days and striving so hard to make her business a success. Jessi was glad that Patti had decided to sell her interior design company and come down here to the Outer Banks. The past two years were probably some of the happiest of her friend's life.

"Want some help?" Allan asked, coming up behind her.

"No."

"Jessi—"

"I'm mad at you. I'm not going to pretend we're okay or anything like that. You might want to go and talk to James and see if he needs your help," she said. There was one thing about being so honest, and that was that she felt freer than she had in a long time. She sort of liked it.

"No."

"What do you mean, no?"

"Just what I said. You changed the rules on me in one second and expected me to keep up with whatever was going on inside of you. That's not fair. Just this morning in the kitchen you walked away instead of staying," he reminded her. "I'm trying to catch up, Jessi. But I'm a guy. And these are emotions, and I'm not even going to pretend that I will ever be comfortable with them. Yes, I have them. No, I never want to talk about them."

She stopped what she was doing and looked up at him. He had his sunglasses on so it was hard to tell if he was sincere. But his words made a lot of sense to her. She had made a radical change of heart and she'd wanted him to immediately catch up to her. In fact, she wondered if she'd been a little bit cowardly by trying to force him to. His reaction had given her the freedom to feel superior and also the safety to back away again.

"I just have no idea what to do with you."

"Me, either," he admitted. "I guess for once we're both in the same place."

"We're always in the same place when we are warring, and I liked that for a long time," she admitted. "But now I want something else. And it scares me because you're still you."

"Yes, I am. But I'll let you in on a little secret.… You

scare me, too. I have no idea how I came to be in this position," Allan said. "I don't like it. I'm going to do everything I can to figure out how to get us back to where I feel comfortable. And it's not because I don't care."

She took his hand and led him from the yard up to the back porch, where they were hidden from the view of the handyman. "I want to know two things…first, where do you feel most comfortable with me, and second, how much do you care?"

"Right here," he said, pulling her into his arms and bringing his mouth down on hers.

It had been too long since they'd kissed and since she'd really held him in her arms. That one-sided hug upstairs hadn't done anything for her. But in his embrace she thought she heard all the things that he couldn't or wouldn't say out loud to her. And it was enough.

She saw this as a first step to something new and exciting. Something worth the scary knot that she felt in her stomach when she looked into the future and thought she saw Allan by her side. It wasn't anything concrete, but she felt as if it was the start of something.

"Uh…excuse me," James said in a gruff voice. "I don't mean to interrupt."

Allan slowly let his arms fall from her, and turned to face the other man. He was about six feet tall, and weathered from a life spent outdoors. His face had sun and laugh lines on it and he wore his faded jeans and work shirt well, as if he was very comfortable with the man he was.

"Yes?" Allan asked.

"There's been a weather update and the storm is confirmed to be heading straight for us. Landfall is in less than four hours. I'm going to go and get the storm shutters to cover the windows. You two should make plans to head off island."

"I'm not sure we can," Allan said. "Until we hear from our attorney."

"I'll get Hannah ready," Jessi said. "And then call Reggie. I also read some stuff on hurricane preparedness, and I've bought water and some nonperishables at the grocery store. Is there anything else I should do, James?"

"Fill the bathtubs with water in case something happens to contaminate the local supply. Also gather a radio, flashlights, candles and that sort of stuff all in one room. I'd pick one without windows."

"Okay," Allan said. "Do you need my help?"

"Yes," James said. "We have to secure everything in the yard and get the windows covered."

Allan squeezed Jessi's hand before he walked away, and she watched him go with a smile in her heart. It didn't matter that a big hurricane—Hurricane Pandora, it was now officially called—was heading straight toward them. Sure, she was scared, but having Allan there to help her reassured her a little because he wasn't the type of person to just sit passively by. She knew there was still so much that had to be settled and figured out between them. But for the first time in her life she had someone by her side.

A man she could count on. It was something that she'd never guessed she'd find. That the man was Allan McKinney was even more surprising, but there it was.

She gathered all the supplies that James had listed, as well as enough diapers for a week, and put them in the small study at the back of the house. The room had bookcases on all the walls and no windows.

She piled up pillows and blankets and a spare bassinet she'd found in Patti's closet for Hannah to sleep in. Then she called the attorney.

"Reggie Blythe's office, this is Reggie," he said.

"It's Jessi Chandler. I was hoping to find out if you'd had an update from the judge," she replied. "We've been told we're going to have to leave the island."

"As I mentioned to Allan, you can't leave with Hannah. It's not allowed until we get the paperwork. The farthest you could go would be to a hotel farther inland—is that what you both want? You can leave her with her foster family, or if you want, stay with her, I'll bring over the notice from the judge so that the police don't try to clear you off. I'm afraid all the judicial offices are sort of shut down while everyone prepares for this storm."

"Should we be scared? Should we go inland?" Jessi asked. "I don't know what to expect."

"I'd stay here. That bed-and-breakfast has weathered many late-season hurricanes. You'll be fine as long as you follow instructions and do what you're told. Do you have enough water and food for a few days?"

"I think so." She thought of the stocked cupboard and cases of water and soda she'd purchased. How much food would they need?

"I'll stop by to check on you," Reggie said.

"That would be nice, but only if you have time. We sort of have a handyman helping us out."

"Very well. I'll call as soon as I hear something from the judge."

Jessi busied herself getting ready for the hurricane

and tried to ignore the storm inside her as she adjusted to everything that was happening. Not the least of which were her feelings for Allan, and that they were all each other had in the coming storm.

She was scared by that, because if she took this gamble with her heart and it didn't pay off, she had the feeling she'd never again take a chance on loving a man.

Twelve

Allan sent Fawkes off island as Hurricane Pandora came toward them. The bed-and-breakfast was secured and they'd done everything possible to get prepared. Now all they could do was wait.

Reggie had finally gotten the judge to sign the papers that gave guardianship to both Jessi and Allan, but it had been too late to leave Hatteras when that happened. The rains had already started falling heavily and the road leading off the island was washed out.

Now they were sitting tensely in the study with a transistor radio on, because the electricity had gone out. They had flashlights and water. For a long time Allan pretended to be reading on his iPad, but the sound of the wind whipping through the yard and the harrowing noise of tree branches scraping against the house distracted him.

Jessi sat on the floor next to a sleeping Hannah.

"I don't like this," she said at last. "It sounds creepy outside and it's so dark and gloomy in here. Distract me, Allan."

"How am I supposed to do that?"

"I don't know. Tell me something about you that no one else knows."

"Okay, and then you'll tell me something?" he asked.

"Sure. Anything is better than listening to the storm," she said.

He got off the couch and came and sat on the floor next to her. "What do you want to know?"

"Tell me about your first kiss," she said. "Ballsy guy like you, it was probably remarkable."

He shook his head. "It was awkward. One of those moments in middle school when I thought I knew everything. It was at Amy Collins's thirteenth birthday party. It was a boy-girl party—a big deal. Her parents were trying to be cool, so they left us all alone in the converted third-floor game room. Jose kept watch at the door while we played spin the bottle, and I got to kiss the birthday girl.

"We went behind a bookcase that held DVDs and stared at each other. Finally, I leaned in and kissed her. Sort of missed her mouth and ended up kissing her cheek and then her mouth. It was over really quickly and both of us looked at each other, wondering if that was it."

Jessi smiled. "My first kiss was sort of like that, too. At a birthday party. Tons of other kids around. Patti liked this boy in our class, but he wasn't about to make a move, so I organized a game of truth or dare, intending to help Patti get her kiss. But instead I got dared to kiss Bobby and I did it. It wasn't bad. A bit like yours, where we sort of smashed mouths and then backed away. Isn't it funny, that age? I felt so ready to be a grown-up, but after that kiss I knew I'd end up waiting before I tried it again. It was scary, letting a boy that close to me."

"I bet. Boys have cooties at that age," Allan said. He had felt energized by the closeness with Amy that day and had become determined to get another kiss, which he had. But as he looked over at Jessi and the sleeping Hannah, he felt differently. "I definitely am not going to be the 'cool' dad where Hannah is concerned. I know how boys are and will keep my eye on anyone that gets too close to her."

Jessi laughed. "Good. You protect her and I'll teach her how to protect herself, in case one slips by us."

"Deal," Allan said.

"Did we just agree on something?" she asked with a smirk.

"No, you're mistaken…. I was about to ask about your tattoo. When did you get it and why?" He liked the intimacy created by the storm raging outside and the quiet ambient light inside. For this moment they were the only two people in the world, and that suited him.

"I got it when I turned eighteen. My parents wouldn't allow me to have one, but on my second day at the University of Texas in Austin I went and had it done anyway. I wanted something to commemorate the fact that I was on my own, free and flying toward the future."

"Why did you get it here?" he asked, touching her collarbone. He liked touching her and used the tattoo as an excuse to do it now.

"I wanted to see it every time I looked in the mirror so I'd remember the promises I made to myself."

"What promises?" he asked.

"That's another question," she said. "And it's my turn to ask."

"I'll tell you whatever you want to know," he said. "Just tell me what promise you made to yourself."

She stared at him for long moments and then shifted up on her knees and leaned forward so that barely an inch separated them. "I promised myself I'd never again let someone make me be something I'm not."

"You certainly have lived up to that," he said.

"It hasn't always been easy. You make it hard for me," she said quietly.

"Good, because you're always keeping me off my guard," he said. "Every time I think I've figured out how to deal with you something changes."

"Ha."

"Ha?"

"That's just a nice way of saying you can't manipulate me," she said.

"Perhaps. But I've discovered I'm not a big fan of manipulating you," he said. It hadn't taken him long to figure out that he wanted the real responses from Jessi instead of the bad-girl attitude she gave everyone else. "What's your question for me?"

She glanced over at Hannah and then moved a little bit closer to him. "Will you answer me truthfully?"

"Yes," he said.

"Then my question is this, Allan McKinney. How long are you going to keep pretending that everything in your world hasn't been changed by the past two weeks?" she asked.

It was a gutsy question and left no doubt as to what she really needed from him. He put his hands on her hips and drew her closer.

But she stopped him with a hand on his chest. "No funny business. I want your answer."

But funny business was the only answer he had. He wasn't going to confess his feelings, which he'd thought he'd made plain to her earlier in the day. Instead, he tangled his fingers in the back of her hair and drew her forward, kissing her with all the emotion that was pent up inside of him.

He cared for this complicated woman who had the ability to make him feel things—things he didn't want to feel. And he wasn't about to let her have the upper hand now.

Something hit the side of the house hard and they pulled back from each other, startled by the sound.

"What was that?" she asked, moving to pick up Hannah.

"I'll go and check," he said. It was impossible to really see through the windows, which had been boarded up, but he knew there was a tiny window near the front door that they had only taped. The handyman had told him the tape would keep the window in one piece, preventing it from shattering if it blew out of the frame.

When Allan got to the front hallway and looked through the window, he saw that a large tree limb had fallen on the front porch. He took a step back as the wind continued whipping branches and other debris down the street

"Are we going to be okay?" Jessi asked from down the hallway, where she held Hannah in her arms.

"Yes," he said. Suddenly, his determination not to show how much she meant to him seemed stupid. Their best friends' death had proved how short life could be, and the storm raging outside seemed a reminder to him to grab on to what was important to him while he still could.

He walked to her and wrapped an arm around her shoulders, leading her into the living room, where he pushed a love seat into the corner, away from the windows, and then gestured for Jessi to sit down. She did, and he settled next to her, wrapping his arm around her and pulling her and Hannah back against his chest.

"I'm not going to let anything hurt you or the baby. I'm going to protect you both," he said. And he repeated that vow inside himself, knowing it was one he'd never break.

"I'm scared," Jessi said. "This storm isn't something I know how to deal with. Plus it lasts so long, not like earthquakes."

"Spoken like a true Californian," he said. "I feel the same way. Give me an earthquake over this any day."

The storm seemed to be getting more intense, and he held her closer, wrapping his arms around both her and Hannah, until he heard Jessi mumbling something under her breath.

"What's that you said?" he asked.

"I'm praying," she said, tipping her head back to make eye contact. "Usually I'm not spiritual at all, but if anything makes me believe in a higher power it's this kind of storm."

"It makes me reprioritize my life, too. Family hasn't really mattered—"

"Yeah, right. You do everything with your cousins," she said.

"That's true, but our bond feels more like one brothers have. We've always been united with a common goal, and no matter what you think, our 'family' has had some problems over the years," Allan said. He'd never wanted to be tied to his cousins other than through the business. But they were friends and they'd shared the bitterness of their grandfather's goals for so long they couldn't be anything else. "What I was trying to say is that I always liked my money and my expensive adult toys, but being here with you and Hannah has made me realize that I can enjoy the quiet things, as well."

"Facing death makes you more accepting of certain things," Jessi murmured.

"Indeed," Allan said.

Jessi went back to her quiet prayers, and he held her and Hannah in his arms, watching over these two females who'd become so important to him in such a short time. He didn't know if these feelings would last beyond the storm or even beyond the time here in North Carolina. But he did know that they were very real and he liked them. He didn't have to talk about it to anyone, and as the storm raged outside, his feelings finally settled down inside.

He didn't need to know anything else at this moment.

"You're quiet," Jessi said.

"Just thinking," he said.

"About?"

"Stuff," he said.

"Stuff…what's that mean? Something weighty or something naughty? I can tell it's a subject you don't want to talk about," she said.

"Then why are you asking me about it?"

"Because I'm nosy and I like needling you."

"You certainly do a very good job of it," he said.

"Thanks."

He squeezed her and dropped a quick kiss on her neck, biting the spot just next to her tattoo. "Keep it up and I might have to give you what you're asking for."

"And that would be?" she asked in that cheeky tone of hers.

"Something naughty," he said.

"I like you when you're naughty," she responded.

"I like you that way, too," he said.

He leaned in close and whispered exactly what it was he would do to her, in detail. He could tell she was interested by the way she settled back against him. He kept talking, seducing her with his words.

He felt a little sad as he realized he'd never met another woman who suited his many sides and his many moods. Jessi's sexual drive was as fierce as his. Her loyalty to her sisters and her company was as laudable as his was. Her closely guarded emotions were hard to ascertain and made her as vulnerable as his did. And he didn't mind right now. At the moment that seemed exactly as it should be.

The worst of the winds seemed to pass a little after midnight, and they decided to sleep in the study with Hannah. The radio was still on and every once in a while they heard something else fly around in the yard. Jessi was feeling so much at this moment that she feared she was going to implode. She was worried and scared, and it seemed her awakening a day ago was timely, because this storm just reinforced that she wanted to live her life and stop being scared of things.

She needed to be more honest with the people who mattered to her, and she vowed once the storm was over she would do just that.

Allan made a quick trip through the house to check on the storm as she got Hannah into bed.

"Jess, come here," he called to her.

She walked down the hall to where he stood at the entrance, where that small window gave them a glimpse of the street and the world in the eye of the storm. He wrapped his arm around her and pointed outside.

"This reminds me that no matter how much research I do there are always going to be situations where I'm not in control," he said.

"It makes me feel small," she said. "And as you saw earlier, makes me believe in God."

"Did you make a bargain with Him?" Allan asked.

She turned in his arms. The faded scent of his aftershave, a fragrance she associated only with him, assailed her senses. "I did."

"I did, too," he said, surprising her.

"What'd you ask for?"

"I told God that if he got us through this then I'd stop…running from life, and give happiness a real shot."

Jessi narrowed her eyes as she watched him. "I don't believe that. Sounds a little too pat."

"Now you're judging what I asked for?" he demanded.

"It's like saying you wanted money when you already have enough," she said. "You haven't run from anything in your life. You stay in place and manipulate everything around you."

He tipped his head to the side and studied her. "You're right, but inside I run away and lock myself in a place where I don't have to engage. You said pretty much that very thing to me earlier."

"Fair enough. I shouldn't have judged. You just always seem so strong and so brave it's hard to think of you as someone who would run from trouble," she said.

"You seem to be the exact same way," he commented.

"You couldn't be further from the truth," she said. "And I promised God that if he kept us all safe I'd be better."

"Better?"

"Yes," she said, "Nicer to my sisters and to you and your cousins. I'd stop being afraid for Hannah and embrace loving her, even though I know that I can't always keep her safe."

Allan didn't say anything, just pulled her close and hugged her so tightly she couldn't breathe. She hugged him back with the same strength. Then she tipped her head up so she could see his face, and the expression on it made her breath catch in her throat.

He'd said earlier that he couldn't express his emotions, but right now there was something stark and raw in his eyes that she couldn't describe as anything other than love. And it awakened that same well of feeling inside her.

"Allan—"

He kissed her, his mouth moving over hers with purpose and she knew that he couldn't talk about whatever was in his heart. But for her it was enough that she'd seen in his eyes the emotions she'd been afraid to admit she wanted from him.

His hands moved over her body, not in a calculated seduction, but in a frenzied burst of passion, and it awakened the exact same frenetic desire in her. She quickly freed his sex from his pants, and he fumbled with her zipper. For the first time since they'd become intimate partners he wasn't smoothly seductive, and that rawness turned her on like nothing else could.

He lifted her and her pants fell to the floor and she shimmied out of her panties before he lifted her again. "Wrap your legs around me."

She did as he asked and felt the world spin as he turned them so her back was against the wall. His mouth captured hers, his tongue plunging deep as he thrust heavily into her. She clenched down hard on him, holding tight to his shoulders with her arms, and his waist with her legs.

He pulled his mouth from hers and kissed his way down the column of her neck, stopping at her tattoo—a spot that she was slowly coming to understand he loved. He laved it with his tongue and then leaned down to kiss and suck there.

Thought left her and instinct took over. With each thrust of his body he drove her closer to her orgasm and made his way deeper into her soul.

There was nothing of the Allan she'd come to expect in this fast coupling. When he lifted his head from her neck, she stared into his silver eyes and watched his pupils dilate as the first wave of her own climax washed over her.

Her orgasm seemed to trigger his and he started thrusting even harder, driving them both to the brink and then over it again as he spilled his seed inside her. It was warm and filled her with his essence.

She didn't even mind that they'd forgotten to use protection. It would have been an intrusion in this moment when their souls had united and their hearts had taken small steps toward each other.

It was not a moment she could regret, because for the first time in her life she felt as if she'd found a man she could depend on. And she was so glad it was Allan McKinney.

Thirteen

The next afternoon, once the winds had subsided, Jessi was glad to get out of the house and away from Allan for a few moments. Neither of them had spoken about what had happened in the hallway or afterward, when he'd carried her back into the living room and they'd fallen asleep in each other's arms, watching over Hannah.

Now that the storm had passed, she knew that everything was going to change. They were cleared to leave Hatteras, and Fawkes was on his way back to the island to help them make arrangements to return to L.A.

She stared outside at the sand that had been pushed up onto the street and into the front yard and the water that hadn't subsided with the tide. It was hard to imagine this place ever getting back to normal.

Downed branches and debris were strewn everywhere she looked. She remembered that howling wind and driving rain and wanted to keep Hannah as far away from this area as she could.

The hurricane had been big and scary. The only thing that had made it tolerable had been Allan, and Jessi was afraid that she was really relying too much on him. He was the man who didn't believe in love. He was the son of her family's sworn rivals. And he was truly the only one that she wanted.

Jessi was surprised when her phone started ringing. The cell towers must already be working again.

"Jess—thank God. Are you okay?" Cari asked when Jessi answered the call. "I've been dialing your number every half hour trying to get you."

She could imagine her younger sister carefully watching the clock and making sure she didn't miss a chance to call. "I'm okay. Allan is assessing the damage, but I think we made it through without too much."

"What was it like?" Cari asked.

"Intense. Loud and scary," Jessi said. "I wouldn't want to go through one again. We can't even drive on the main road. We have to walk everywhere."

"You won't have to once you come home. You're staying here, right?" her sister asked.

"Of course. Why wouldn't I?"

"I didn't know if you'd decided you'd had enough with the gaming world and wanted a change."

"No. My life is there. And I am working toward my objectives to satisfy my probation. I'm pretty sure I'll be joining you on the safe list soon," Jessi said. There was no way that securing a big money deal with a Hollywood producer wouldn't save her, and she had managed to reschedule the meeting with Jack White before the full force of the hurricane hit.

"Emma said you're on the cut list. Something about missing a deadline yesterday," Cari told her.

"What are you talking about? There was a hurricane and all the communications were down on the island. Hell, the entire southern Atlantic Seaboard was cut off," Jessi said.

"I know. Believe me, I think it's ridiculous and I've already raised my objection. If Kell doesn't back down I'm going to take it to the board."

"Fat lot of good that will do you," Jessi said. "I'm sure…I'll figure it out. Rest assured, I'm going to be back home to stay."

"Good. I miss you. And I really want to get to know little Hannah. She is so cute," Cari said. "Are you adjusting to being a mommy?"

"No," Jessi said bluntly. "I love her and I am doing stuff for her like I should, but it doesn't feel natural to me. I still hesitate before I do everything. I'm afraid I'll screw up."

"That's just part of being a parent," Cari said. "We all get overwhelmed sometimes.

"Emma doesn't feel like that," Jessi said.

"Emma's not human. She's a perfect oldest child who exists solely to make us feel inadequate," Cari said with a laugh.

"It seems that way sometimes," Jessi agreed, glancing at herself in the mirror. She had on a pair of artfully faded designer jeans with rips in the knees, and a silk blouse that she'd tied at her left hip. She'd put the combat boots on because walking in debris was going to be tricky.

As she glanced at her own reflection she admitted to herself she hardly looked like a mom. But inside she felt fiercely protective of Hannah, and she knew that moms came in all kinds of packages.

"Thanks for calling, Cari," she said.

"I love you, Jessi. I miss you and I was very worried about you."

"We were safe from the hurricane. I think this house has been standing for a long time, and John made sure to keep it up-to-date regarding hurricane codes."

"That's not why I was worried. You haven't been yourself lately. You've been a lot…harder than normal."

Harder. She knew what her sister meant and it just reinforced what she'd discovered recently: that no matter how well she thought she was doing at making the world think she was doing okay, she wasn't fooling anyone. "Life's been tough lately."

"Yes, it has," Cari agreed. "Doesn't seem fair that Grandfather sowed all this bad karma and we're the ones who are reaping it."

"No, it doesn't," Jessi said. "But no one ever said life was fair."

"It should be," Cari insisted. "We will do our best to make sure it is. I'm going to camp out in Kell's office until he agrees to take your name off the cut list."

"Thanks, little sis, but that's not for you to do. I already have a meeting scheduled that will change his mind. It's funny to me that a big-shot Hollywood producer understood that I had to reschedule due to Mother Nature, but the CEO of a gaming company couldn't," Jessi said.

"Kell hates us more than a normal person should," Cari said. "He's not all bad, though. He is nice to D.J."

"He's probably secretly brainwashing him to hate us," Jessi said.

"Jess—that's not true. I've got to go. I have a meeting in a few minutes. Love you."

"Love you, too," Jessi said, disconnecting the call.

She couldn't believe that Kell was being so stubborn about that timeline he'd developed. Did he really hate her so much? She'd hardly met the man. Was he that bitter just because of her last name?

She wasn't too worried, though. She'd win Jack White over, and surely after all they'd been through together Allan would be on her side. He had some sway over his cousin. She knew that and expected him to use it to help her.

And the two of them had a new bond. One that was stronger than ever. She felt confident that the man she'd spent the past tense night with was on her side. She knew she'd seen love in his eyes, and there was no way that someone who was in love would let his partner be hurt.

Partner… That almost sounded scarier than being in love. Was Allan her partner now? Did they have a true bond that would make them both stronger? Or was she kidding herself again? All her doubts made her feel small and insecure, and she wasn't going to give in to them. She couldn't.

She had to believe in Allan and in herself.

Allan had never seen this many downed limbs or this much standing water. It was the first time he'd seen damage like this. He'd grown up with mudslides and fires, but this was different. And the storm last night had been so loud…so intense. They were lucky the bed-and-breakfast was still standing.

He continued walking around the yard and searching for damage. He felt glad that now that the storm was over, he could get out of North Carolina. Frankly, he was ready to get away from Jessi.

Last night had been intense. He'd never been more alive, never felt every sense come awake like that. But this morning, with the sun shining down from the clear blue sky, he felt too exposed. Too vulnerable to the one person in the world he needed to be the strongest around.

He looked down at Hannah as she kicked her arms and legs in the carrier he was using to keep her with him as he surveyed the land. She seemed in good spirits this morning, and he had to admit the baby was a joy.

But at the same time he was always a little scared to let himself care for her. If things got sour between Jessi and him, one of them was going to have to give up their rights to the baby. Him, he thought. It was the perfect out. An easy way to hide from the emotions he felt toward both of them. He wasn't sure he could handle being that vulnerable. Both of them made him weak.

And though the judge had granted guardianship to both of them, in the back of his mind Allan was braced for the moment when he might lose Hannah. Lose them both.

If his life had followed one pattern, it was that no one he cared about stayed around forever. His mom had left; his dad had followed by taking his own life. His grandfather had been distant; Allan had never been close to the bitter old man. He was close to his cousins, but they all lived their own lives and went their own way.

Better that he make the break now before he let them both any deeper into his life and his heart.

And then there was John. John was probably the final blow, in that he was the one person who'd known Allan best. The one person he'd trusted to have his back. And now he was gone.

Why then would this little girl be any different? Or for that matter, Jessi? They'd both tried to make the situation between them into one that they could live with, but they both knew they were too different.

Last night, with a storm raging outside and that feeling that the world was just the three of them, it had made sense to let his guard down and make love to Jessi. Really make love. They'd had sex prior to that, but last night he'd felt as if he could almost let the full force of his emotions free. And now today…that seemed stupid.

It seemed like the move of a man who didn't know how to control himself or his own future. And that was a mistake. He just wished he had a solid plan for fixing the situation.

He was going to have to handle things carefully or he'd leave himself open to a lot of hurt and pain from Jessi. And a part of him almost believed he might deserve that. A part of him last night had been swept away by things…dreams that he knew he'd never really attain. They weren't things he really wanted, no matter how much he thought he might have in that moment.

"Looks like the bed-and-breakfast weathered the storm pretty well," James said, coming up to him. The handyman had called earlier to say he'd come by and help take down the storm shutters.

"It did. This building is certainly sturdy," Allan said.

"Yes, it is. John did a lot of work on it before Patti came down here. That man just wanted to keep her safe," James said.

"There are no guarantees in life," Allan stated.

"That's true enough. I've been meaning to talk to you about something that Jessi mentioned," James said.

"Yes?"

"You still looking for a caretaker to keep the inn open?"

"Yes, we are. I've asked Reggie Blythe, the McCoys' attorney, to help in the search," Allan said.

"Well, I talked to the wife and we'd like a chance at the job," James said.

Allan liked the idea of James and his wife taking over the inn until Hannah was old enough to decide what she wanted to do with it. "I'll tell Reggie, and then we can get him to draw up a contract and all that."

"Sounds good," the handyman said.

"Allan?" Jessi called from the front porch. She sounded troubled. "Can I talk to you?"

"Go on then," James told him. "I can get the storm shutters down by myself and store them."

"Thanks," Allan said.

"No problem," he replied.

Allan walked toward the house and noticed that Hannah waved her arms as they got closer. He wondered if she recognized Jessi. The book had said that she should start doing so at this age.

"What's up?"

"Um…your cousin still has me on the cut list, supposedly because I missed a deadline yesterday."

"I haven't had a chance to talk to him," Allan said. "The lines have been down all morning. Do you have a signal on your cell?"

"Yes. Cari called me," Jessi said. "So you don't know anything about this?"

"No, I don't," Allan said. He was angry on her behalf, until he realized that if he played this on Kell's side Jessi would back away from him. He'd be left alone, but it might be better given the fact that he couldn't see a way for them to really move forward from this, except as coguardians of the child and nothing more.

He wasn't prepared to let Jessi be his heart and soul every day for the rest of his life. He wasn't sure he could exist, feeling that insecure and vulnerable. As James had just said, no matter how much a man tried to protect the ones he loved, somehow when fate wanted them, they'd always be taken.

"Let's go inside and discuss this," Allan said. He walked past her, taking Hannah from the carrier he wore and transferring her to his arms. For a moment Jessi just watched him and tried to keep herself from feeling so in love with him. He was all the things she'd hoped to find in a man, but had never wanted to admit she'd been searching for.

He handed Hannah to her while he took off the carrier, and then went into the kitchen to wash his hands and pour himself some sweet tea.

She followed him and watched, waiting for him to call Kell. But it soon became apparent he wasn't going to.

"Aren't you going to call your cousin and chew his ass out for not taking me off the cut list?" Jessi said when he went to pour himself a second glass of sweet tea.

"No. Listen, Jessi, I understand your point, but Kell has one; as well. In business there are deadlines and they have to be met. That's how successful companies stay successful."

"I'm not saying I shouldn't have to meet the objectives laid out for me, but when there's a hurricane I think even Kell Montrose will have to admit it's impossible to do business."

"Yeah, but Kell won't."

"What about you, Allan? Will you?"

"Will I what?"

"Back me up. Support me. That's what I really need from you in this," Jessi said. She went to the fridge as Hannah started to get a little fussy and took out a bottle she'd prepared earlier. After heating it up, she gave it to the baby and stared at Allan, waiting to hear what he had to say.

But Allan was simply standing there, watching her.

"You're a good mother," he said.

"Thank you, Allan. I really did need to hear that," she said. "I'm learning, but I'm nowhere near where I need to be, and I don't want to talk about mothering right now. I'm still trying to figure out if you're in my corner or not. I thought we had each other's backs last night in the storm...."

Allan scrubbed his hand over his face and turned his back to her, putting his palms on the countertop in front of him and lowering his head. She wasn't asking much from him, so couldn't really understand his reaction.

"I just want to know you're on my side," she said again, and then realized that his continued silence was his answer. "You're not, are you?"

"I am just saying that, legally, Kell's not in the wrong here."

"We're not talking about Kell. We're talking about you and me. And if you feel what I do, then the answer is simple. You should want what's best for me. Even though you are being a complete ass right now I still care for you, Allan. I'd still defend you."

"That's good to know. I've never had you in my corner," he said.

She literally started shaking as his words sank in. Anger swept over her and she was livid. "I can't believe you're going to be flip about this. The last few weeks have been intense. They've changed my life and made me see things in a completely new way.

"I thought last night when we talked we shared something deep and meaningful, and yet right now you're acting like nothing has changed at all between us," she said.

She had to put Hannah in her baby chair with her bottle, because she didn't feel steady as her emotions got the better of her.

He turned back around to face her, but quickly averted his eyes. "Calm down," he said.

"Don't say that to me," she retorted. "I am calm. I just need answers from you."

"Well, I don't know what to say. Our time together has been intense, but it's not real. We both know that our lives are in California, and no matter what I might say to the contrary we are too different from each other to have a relationship. These days have been great and I'll treasure them always, but this has no meaning in our real lives. No matter how much I want to pretend otherwise."

"Pretend?" she repeated. She let his words sink in for a moment and then shook her head. "Last night I thought I saw the real man. The man behind the big gestures and the witty banter. Last night I had a glimpse of a man who was strong not by waving around his money or whisking people to places they've never visited, but with the quiet strength to know that all he needed was the right people by his side."

"There is an element of truth to that," he admitted. "I do lo—care for you. It's just that we've been living under a very intense set of circumstances. This isn't real. I can't pretend it is and neither can you."

"We weren't pretending last night. Or at least I wasn't," she said.

"Last night we thought we'd die in the house. Today…"

"Today you are showing yourself to be the man I guess you are, Allan. You're a coward. I never thought you'd be so shady. No matter how much we butted heads I always had a sort of grudging respect for you. The way you cared about John and your cousins, I thought you were a man with a heart. A man who would be worthy of not only my admiration, but also my love. Yet I see now that you're nothing but a hollow shell of a man."

"Is that all?" he asked, crossing his arms over his chest.

"Yes, it is," she said. "I'm taking Hannah back home as soon as I can get off the island. We'll work out a visitation schedule through our lawyers."

Still she hesitated, waiting to see if he'd stop her from leaving, and maybe ask her to stay. But he didn't. Instead, he just nodded at her.

"That makes sense. I'm going to stay here and settle things with the insurance company. Luckily, there wasn't as much storm damage as there could have been. I'll contact you when I'm back in California. Unless you have any objections, I've decided to hire James as the caretaker for the bed-and-breakfast."

She shook her head. "You really are all about yourself, aren't you? I thought I got a glimpse of a man who wasn't so shallow, but it seems I was wrong."

Picking up Hannah, she left the kitchen and her broken heart behind. She'd known from the moment they'd met that he wasn't all he pretended to be. But a part of her had hoped she was wrong, and she was really upset at herself for believing in the illusion of Allan McKinney.

Fourteen

Jessi didn't have any time to sleep after she got back to California. Her sisters met her at LAX and they went straight to her house. As they sat on the patio catching up, Jessi started to have a new vision of herself rising out of the ashes of her humiliating confession to Allan.

"Can one of you watch Hannah for me this afternoon?" she asked.

"Of course," Cari said. "Why?"

"I've got that meeting with Jack White, and even though the Montrose cousins are busy acting like I've shirked my responsibilities, I'm going to go through with it and deliver what I said I would."

"I'll go with you," Emma said.

"Why?"

"Because you'll need someone to make sure the financials make sense. Kell will crucify you if they aren't solid. It's your deal. I'll just be there to verify things," her big sister said.

"Thanks," Jessi replied, going back to staring out at the Pacific. It was a beautifully sunny day here, and on the outside, it seemed as if nothing had changed. But inside she was aching. Aching for Allan, which made her angrier than she'd expected. She had to admit that it was anger and hurt that were really driving her right now. She wanted to do what she could to prove to herself to the Montrose heirs, but most especially to Allan, who'd been too much of a coward—

Stop it, she reminded herself. She wasn't going to let herself go down that path again.

"Tell us more about what happened in North Carolina," Cari said.

"There's not much more to say," Jessi answered. "It was tough dealing with Patti's funeral and checking in on her mom. And then that hurricane…I don't think I ever want to experience anything like that again."

"What about Allan? Did something happen between the two of you?"

"No," she said.

"Liar," Emma declared. "You look like Cari did when she was pretending that Dec was nothing to her or D.J. You can't fool us. What really happened with Allan?"

Jessi looked over at her big sister and suddenly felt as if she were eight again. Back then, she might have been the one to defend Cari, but Emma had always been the one who defended Jessi. "I fell for him, but he didn't feel the same. I screwed up and now I'm just trying to survive."

"Oh, sweetie," Cari said.

Emma got up, came around to where Jessi sat and wrapped her arms around her.

"Love sucks." Jessi sighed.

"Yes, it does," she agreed.

Emma's husband had been killed in a car crash. He'd

been a Formula One driver and had been ripped from Emma's life while she'd been pregnant with their son.

"It's worse for you," Jessi said. "I'm just being a baby."

"It's not worse for either of us. When you fall in love with someone and they aren't in your life anymore, whether they are deceased or not it hurts. And you just have to learn to move on from it," Emma said.

"How, Emmy? How am I supposed to do that? I've never let myself care about a man like this. I've always kept it light."

"It's different for each of us," she murmured. "I kept Helio's obituary on my nightstand and reread it any time I thought I'd just imagined that he was gone."

Jessi hugged her sister back. Emma always seemed so strong that it was shocking to hear how vulnerable she had been.

"What changed for you?" Cari asked. "Why did you let Allan in?"

"I didn't mean to. I guess I could blame it on Hannah, but the truth is, I've been restless for a while. The Playtone takeover made me realize how life was changing and so were my priorities. But honestly, I didn't mean to fall for Allan. He's good-looking and all that, but he can be an ass."

"You would know better than either of us," Cari said. "He's always been pretty nice to me."

Emma glared at Cari.

"I still hate him for what he did to you, Jess."

Jessi had to smile at her sisters rallying around her. And it drove home something that she'd been completely unaware of her entire life. She'd thought she was the rebel and the loner, but she'd overlooked the fact that her sisters always had her back. It didn't matter if they held a differing opinion on things or if they were fighting about something else—when the chips were down they were always by her side.

"Thanks, girls," she said, smiling at both of them. In the corner on a blanket she heard Sam talking quietly to his little cousins. She reflected on how two years ago there had been only the three Chandler sisters, but now there was a future generation. Jessi needed no further proof that life just kept moving on no matter how much you felt like checking out from it.

"You're welcome. But what did we do?" Cari asked with a smile. Her youngest sister had such a good, open heart that Jessi had thought she was weak at times. But the past few weeks had changed that, and now Jessi understood the true strength that came from loving someone. Hannah had shown her that, and even though she hated to admit it, so had Allan.

"You just reminded me that I'm not alone. And that no matter how many times I might have thought I was, you were both always here for me." Jessi stopped herself before she turned truly sappy and way too emotional. But after all those years of thinking she wasn't a good Chandler girl like Emma and Cari, she finally accepted that that was exactly who she was.

"Of course we were," Emma said. "We're sisters and blood is thicker than water."

"And more trustworthy than men," Jessi said.

She saw the doubt in Cari's eyes, but her youngest sister was in the first throes of a new love.

"You're the exception that proves the rule," Emma said to Cari.

"I don't want to be. I want you each to find a man

who loves you as much as Dec loves me, a man who makes you happy."

Jessi wished she could believe there was a man like that out there waiting for her, but she knew there wasn't. She was fickle in her emotions, and as Emma had said, getting over loving someone was hard. Jessi had the feeling she might never truly stop loving Allan, or being mad at him for not loving her back.

Allan looked around the boardroom at his cousins, but didn't join them in their small talk about the NBA scores. He had never felt emptier than he had since Jessi walked out of his life. And it was his own fault. He'd let her go. Hell, he had encouraged her to leave, thinking that if it was a clean break it would be easier. But he'd been wrong.

He'd never in all his days felt such pain as he did when he woke up every morning alone. He'd been avoiding her ever since he got back to L.A. because a few days earlier he needed to find out if he'd been successful in cleansing her from his soul.

God, he was starting to sound pathetic even to himself. He just knew that he missed her. He didn't want to, but there it was. And the fact that he was going to be able to see her today was the only thing that had made him come into the office. He'd been working from home, getting scruffier by the day and turning into a miserable hermit.

Next week he'd have Hannah with him for the first time since his return, and even that hadn't been enough to stir him from his malaise.

"Allan?"

"Hmm?"

"Snap out of it," Kell said. "I don't know what happened to you in North Carolina, but you've been acting strange since you got back, and I need you sharp and on the ball. I think Jessi is up to something. She was vague when she asked for this meeting, but determined that we all be here."

"She was pissed off the last time I saw her. I'm not sure why she wanted us all here," Allan said, and then thought about it long and hard. So much had changed since the hurricane almost a month ago. It felt as if a lifetime had passed them both by, and now he was faced with a new life. One in which Jessi wasn't his enemy, but was his—what? The answer eluded him and he knew today he had to figure it out. "I bet she's done something to prove us wrong, Kell. She's a fighter and we both backed her into a corner. She's coming out swinging."

"You think so?" Dec asked. The other cousin stood by the window looking out at the sunny October day.

"I know so," Allan said. For the first time since she'd walked out of his life he realized he felt a charge of energy coming back through him. He'd missed her more than he wanted to admit, but he also missed sparring with her. There was so much to Jessi that he had needed, and he'd let her go. "I was a fool."

"Probably," Dec said. "Your name is mud at my house."

"Cari hates me?" Allan asked. She was the sweetest of the three sisters, and he hadn't thought she was capable of disliking anyone.

"I don't think she has it in her to hate. But she's very mad at you and said she pities you."

Nice. Jessi's sisters probably knew all about him.

Knew that he'd been afraid to take a chance on loving her.

"What the hell happened down there?" Kell asked.

"We got close," Allan said.

"Close? Did you fall for her?"

"Obviously," Allan said. "But you don't have to worry about that. I backed you and stayed true to my roots as a Montrose heir."

At what cost? he asked himself. He'd known all along that he was just using Kell and the family feud as an excuse to keep her at arm's length, and now he knew he'd acted like a fool. He had wanted Jessi from the first moment they'd met. It was ridiculous to pretend now that he hadn't.

"Thanks for your loyalty," Kell said. "I know I've made things difficult for both of you."

"You have, but we started this journey together," Allan said. "I'm not cut out to share my life with someone. Not even a woman like Jessi."

"I don't know about that. Our fathers weren't exactly solid examples of how to love a woman and be happy," Dec said.

There was a knock at the door. "Can we continue this conversation later?" Kell asked irritably.

"Come in," Allan called out.

The door opened, and Jessi walked in, but Allan hardly recognized her. Her normally spikey hair was tamed into a sedate style and she wore a suit. A gray-and-cream-checked business suit that made it seem to him as if all the light had gone out of his Jessi. She wore proper makeup, too—no outrageous cat eyes or bright purple lipstick. She was subdued.

He'd done this to her, he thought. He'd killed that rebellious light inside of her with his words on Hatteras. By saying that what they'd experienced together was fueled by circumstance instead of real emotion.

Suddenly, all his fears disappeared, as he acknowledged to himself that she was *his* Jessi. And he wasn't a coward as she'd said. He didn't run away from something he wanted; he claimed it, and he intended to claim her. He tried to catch her eye, but she refused to look his way.

But as the meeting went on and she made her presentation about the deal she'd hammered out with Jack White over the past few weeks to make games out of his latest movie trilogy, Allan knew he'd lost her. She was cold and icy in the meeting room. When any of them asked a question she answered it in a calm, quiet voice and ignored him.

Allan was afraid he'd realized his mistake too late. That he'd never be able to win her back. But when she'd concluded her presentation she gave a quick peek over at him. If he'd blinked he'd have missed it, but it was enough to convince him she was still in love with him. She had to be. Jessi wasn't fickle and wouldn't be able to love lightly.

"We'll have to review this, but we'll get back to you shortly," Kell said.

"Of course," Jessi said, standing up and leaving the room without another word.

Allan reached for the folder in front of Kell, started skimming the numbers and saw that it was a solid business case. Jessi had done more than he'd dreamed she would, and he was impressed anew at her talents. She was strong and smart and sexy and a million other things that he couldn't name just then because he felt such a strong outpouring of love for her. All he could say was, "This is beyond what we asked of her."

"I know. I think we're going to have to offer her a role in the newly merged company," Kell said.

"Um…would you mind doing me a favor?" Allan asked. "I think it could take me months to win her back without a little help from you guys."

"Just tell us what you need," Dec said.

"Am I going to have any cousins-in-law that aren't Chandlers?" Kell asked, but there was a faint grin around his mouth.

"No," Allan said impatiently. "Will you just tell her that you'll have the decision for her tonight, and ask her to return at seven?"

"Okay," Dec said, going out to talk to Jessi.

Allan was energized with a plan and knew exactly what he had to do to win back the only woman he wanted by his side for the rest of his life.

Jessi wasn't sure what the big deal was on the decision, or why she had to come back to the Playtone offices at seven that night, but since the Montrose heirs held all the cards, she did as they asked.

She felt battered from seeing Allan today. She'd thought she'd had control over her emotions. That she'd finally gotten him out of her heart, but she knew now that would never happen.

The love she'd hoped was temporary was starting to feel like the real thing. And keeping a job where she was going to be forced to see him, well, it was tempting. She hated that inside she was so weak where he was concerned, but that was the truth of it. She liked

Allan McKinney and she wanted to see him every day even if it was just at work.

Cari was babysitting Hannah for her tonight, and when Jessi parked her BMW convertible in the parking lot she admitted to herself how hard it had been to be in the same room with Allan and not look at him this afternoon. But she was glad she'd resisted all but that one little glance, which had made her breath catch and her heart beat faster.

She wasn't any closer to falling out of love with him than she'd been on the first day she arrived back in California. In fact, if her racing heart had indicated anything this afternoon, she might be even more in love with him.

She was still mad at him, and realistic enough to know that he was never going to return her feelings, but that hadn't changed anything inside her. She had no idea how she was going to handle things next week, when she had to meet up with him to give him Hannah. Maybe she'd just send Emma with the baby instead of going herself.

Her sister would do it for her. Emma had been in full-on big-sister mode since Jessi had returned from North Carolina, and right now Jessi was wallowing in it. But that had to stop. She was hiding and letting her emotions get the better of her.

Whatever they told her tonight about her job, she was going to have to figure out how to get Allan out of her mind and out of her heart so she didn't raise Hannah to be just as pitiful when it came to love.

Jessi got out of the car and walked into the office building, expecting to find a security guard waiting for her. But instead there stood Allan.

His hair was still as thick as ever and brushed the

back of his collar now. He wore a stylishly slim-cut black suit with a narrow gray tie. But he looked tired, and for the first time since she'd known him he watched her carefully before talking.

"I guess you guys decided to fire me if you're here," she commented when he didn't say anything.

"Don't jump to conclusions," he said.

"Oh, believe me, I don't do that anymore," she stated.

He cursed under his breath.

"Do you trust me?" he asked her.

She could only stare at him, but then took a deep breath. "You want the truth?"

"Always," he said.

She nodded. "I trust you. I trust you to break my heart and to let me down."

"God, Jessi. That's not true. I never wanted to break your heart. How could I?"

She didn't answer that.

"I'm sorry," he said. "I should never have let you leave North Carolina under those circumstances, but I was afraid. You were right when you said that we'd changed in those weeks we were out there together. And the truth was I wasn't ready for us to be different. I was still dealing with the loss of my best friend and finding out that the one woman I'd always thought I hated was actually the woman I loved."

She listened to his words, hoping he was sincere, but then she remembered that Allan was always honest when he spoke. She felt a spark of hope when he closed the gap between them and went down on one knee in front of her.

"I'm begging you, Jess, please forgive me and give me another chance."

She stared down at him as a million thoughts ran through her mind, images of the two of them from the moment they'd met. There had been something between them from the very beginning, and it had taken their friends' deaths to force them both to look at each other in a different way.

"I've missed you, too. I think I got too used to our morning routines and just talking to you during the day."

"I'm sorry I didn't say something to you before. But I didn't want to admit I'd been wrong about so much."

"But you hurt me, Allan. And I'm not the kind of person who likes that emotional pain."

"I won't do it again," he vowed. "I love you, Jess. I thought if I didn't say the words then I couldn't be vulnerable to you, but that wasn't true."

She felt silly standing while he was kneeling at her feet, so she got down on her knees in front of him and wrapped her arms around his big shoulders and kissed him. "I'll give you a second chance, but if you screw up again…"

"I won't," he said, kissing her and running his hands through her hair. "Will you promise me something?"

"Maybe. Depends on what you want."

"I want you to be you. No more suits like this, okay?"

She laughed. "Okay."

They got to their feet. "I have something else to show you."

He led the way to the elevator and took her up to the boardroom where his cousins and her sisters waited. There was a banner with her name on it that said Congratulations.

"Welcome to Playtone-Infinity Games," Kell said. "You hit one out of the park for us."

"Thanks. You didn't make it easy."

"Nothing worth having ever is," Kell said.

Everyone took turns congratulating her, and Jessi felt as if she finally had something she'd always been searching for when she watched Allan take Hannah from Cari. He held the baby in one arm and her with the other. She had a man she could count on, sisters she loved and a family of her own making.

"Just one more thing," Allan said.

"What now?" Jessi asked.

He took a box from his pocket and handed it to her. "Will you marry me?"

She stared at him. Dammit, he'd surprised her and gotten the upper hand, and the grin on his face said he knew it.

"Yes, I'll marry you," she said.

* * * * *

If you loved Jessi's story,
don't miss her sister's tale,

HIS INSTANT HEIR

Available now from USA TODAY *bestselling author*
Katherine Garbera
and Harlequin Desire!

COMING NEXT MONTH FROM

HARLEQUIN®

Desire

Available March 4, 2014

#2287 THE REAL THING
The Westmorelands • by Brenda Jackson
To help Dr. Trinity Matthews fend off unwanted advances at work, Adrian Westmoreland poses as her boyfriend. But when their pretend kisses turn serious, Adrian wants a chance at the real thing.

#2288 THE TEXAS RENEGADE RETURNS
Texas Cattleman's Club: The Missing Mogul
by Charlene Sands
After regaining his memories, rancher Alex del Toro is determined to reclaim the woman he loves—in spite of their families' interference. But then he learns she's been keeping a little secret....

#2289 DOUBLE THE TROUBLE
Billionaires and Babies • by Maureen Child
When his ex-wife falls ill, Colt King discovers he's the father of two adorable twins. Now this unsure father is falling in love all over again—with his ex *and* their babies!

#2290 SEDUCING HIS PRINCESS
Married by Royal Decree • by Olivia Gates
Seducing the princess is Mohab's biggest mission impossible. Overcoming past deceptions and present heartaches, he vows to take her from fake engagement to temporary marriage to...forever.

#2291 SUDDENLY EXPECTING
by Paula Roe
One night with his best friend, Sophie, and Marco Corelli can't get enough. Then, when they're trapped on his private island, Marco gets more than he expected...because Sophie's pregnant!

#2292 ONE NIGHT, SECOND CHANCE
The Hunter Pact • by Robyn Grady
After a sizzling one-night stand, Wynn Hunter is shocked to see his beautiful, nameless stranger again—and to learn exactly who she is! This time, he won't let her get away!

YOU CAN FIND MORE INFORMATION ON UPCOMING HARLEQUIN® TITLES, FREE EXCERPTS AND MORE AT WWW.HARLEQUIN.COM.

HDCNM0214

REQUEST YOUR FREE BOOKS!
2 FREE NOVELS PLUS 2 FREE GIFTS!

ALWAYS POWERFUL, PASSIONATE AND PROVOCATIVE

YES! Please send me 2 FREE Harlequin Desire® novels and my 2 FREE gifts (gifts are worth about $10). After receiving them, if I don't wish to receive any more books, I can return the shipping statement marked "cancel." If I don't cancel, I will receive 6 brand-new novels every month and be billed just $4.55 per book in the U.S. or $4.99 per book in Canada. That's a savings of at least 13% off the cover price! It's quite a bargain! Shipping and handling is just 50¢ per book in the U.S. and 75¢ per book in Canada.* I understand that accepting the 2 free books and gifts places me under no obligation to buy anything. I can always return a shipment and cancel at any time. Even if I never buy another book, the two free books and gifts are mine to keep forever.

225/326 HDN F4ZC

Name   (PLEASE PRINT)

Address   Apt. #

City   State/Prov.   Zip/Postal Code

Signature (if under 18, a parent or guardian must sign)

Mail to the **Harlequin®** Reader Service:
IN U.S.A.: P.O. Box 1867, Buffalo, NY 14240-1867
IN CANADA: P.O. Box 609, Fort Erie, Ontario L2A 5X3

Want to try two free books from another line?
Call 1-800-873-8635 or visit www.ReaderService.com.

* Terms and prices subject to change without notice. Prices do not include applicable taxes. Sales tax applicable in N.Y. Canadian residents will be charged applicable taxes. Offer not valid in Quebec. This offer is limited to one order per household. Not valid for current subscribers to Harlequin Desire books. All orders subject to credit approval. Credit or debit balances in a customer's account(s) may be offset by any other outstanding balance owed by or to the customer. Please allow 4 to 6 weeks for delivery. Offer available while quantities last.

Your Privacy—The Harlequin® Reader Service is committed to protecting your privacy. Our Privacy Policy is available online at www.ReaderService.com or upon request from the Harlequin Reader Service.

We make a portion of our mailing list available to reputable third parties that offer products we believe may interest you. If you prefer that we not exchange your name with third parties, or if you wish to clarify or modify your communication preferences, please visit us at www.ReaderService.com/consumerchoice or write to us at Harlequin Reader Service Preference Service, P.O. Box 9062, Buffalo, NY 14269. Include your complete name and address.

HD13R

SPECIAL EXCERPT FROM

 HARLEQUIN®

Desire

Harlequin® Desire is proud to present

THE REAL THING, a new **Westmoreland** story

by *New York Times* and *USA TODAY* bestselling author

Brenda Jackson

*L*et the show begin, Adrian thought as he stared deep into Trinity's eyes. He could sense her nervousness. Although she had gone along with her sister's suggestion that they pretend to be lovers, he had a feeling she wasn't 100 percent on board with the idea.

Although the man Trinity was trying to avoid was going about it all wrong, Adrian could understand Dr. Belvedere wanting her. Hell, what man in his right mind wouldn't? Trinity was an incredibly beautiful woman. *Ravishing* didn't even come close to describing her.

He recalled the reaction of almost every single man in the room when Trinity had shown up at Riley's wedding. That was when he'd heard she would be moving to Denver for two years to work at a local hospital.

"Are you sure it's him?" Trinity asked, breaking into his thoughts.

"Pretty positive," Adrian said, studying her features. She had creamy mahogany-colored skin, silky black hair that hung to her shoulders and the most gorgeous pair of light brown eyes he'd ever seen. "And it's just the way I planned it," he said.

She raised an arched brow. "The way you planned it?"

"Yes. After your sister called and told me about her idea, I decided to get on it right away. I found out from a reliable source that Belvedere frequents this place, especially on Thursday nights."

"So that's why you suggested we have dinner here tonight?" she asked.

"Yes, that's the reason. The plan is for him to see us together, right?"

"Yes. I just wasn't prepared to run into him tonight. Hopefully, all it will take is for him to see us together and—"

"Back off? Don't bank on that. The man wants you and, for some reason, he feels he has every right to have you. Getting him to leave you alone won't be easy. We should really do something to get his attention."

"What?"

"Just follow my lead."

And then Adrian leaned in and kissed her lips.

Will this pretend relationship turn into something real?
Find out in
THE REAL THING
by New York Times *and* USA TODAY *bestselling author*
Brenda Jackson
Available March 2014
Only from Harlequin® Desire

HARLEQUIN®

Desire

ALWAYS POWERFUL, PASSIONATE AND PROVOCATIVE.

USA TODAY **bestselling author Olivia Gates is back with a scorching tale of power and passion, honor and love in her acclaimed marriage-of-convenience series**

There is only one woman for Mohab Aal Ghaanem, Saraya's top secret service agent. He lost her once, but the promise of peace between two feuding kingdoms could bring Jala Aal Masood back to him—as his wife.

Marry *Mohab?* Six years ago, the Saraya prince risked his life to save Jala's. He awoke irresistible desire…only to destroy her trust. Now royal decree commands the Judar princess make the ultimate sacrifice by giving herself to Mohab. Will fresh heartbreak be her destiny? Or is this her second chance with the man she never stopped loving?

Look for
SEDUCING HIS PRINCESS next month,
from Harlequin® Desire!

Wherever books and ebooks are sold.

Don't miss other scandalous titles from the
Married by Royal Decree miniseries, available now!

TEMPORARILY HIS PRINCESS
by Olivia Gates

CONVENIENTLY HIS PRINCESS
by Olivia Gates

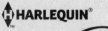

HARLEQUIN®

Desire

ALWAYS POWERFUL, PASSIONATE AND PROVOCATIVE.

What happens in Vegas…

It had been years since Colton King ended his marriage to Penny Oaks. He'd declared their whirlwind Las Vegas nuptials over after just one day. The dedicated businessman had tried to erase her from his memory. Then he discovered Penny had been keeping a huge secret.
Actually two little secrets—a baby boy and a baby girl.

Now this unsure father is falling in love all over again—is he prepared to prove he can be all she needs?

Look for DOUBLE THE TROUBLE
by Maureen Child next month.

Don't miss other scandalous titles from the
Billionaires and Babies miniseries, available now!

YULETIDE BABY SURPRISE
by Catherine Mann

CLAIMING HIS OWN
by Elizabeth Gates

A BILLIONAIRE FOR CHRISTMAS
by Janice Maynard

THE NANNY'S SECRET
by Elizabeth Lane

SNOWBOUND WITH A BILLIONAIRE
by Jules Bennett

HD73302